My Lunatic Life

Book one of *My Lunatic Life* Series

by

Sharon Sala

Bell Bridge Books

Copyright

Bell Bridge Books
PO BOX 300921
Memphis, TN 38130
ISBN: 978-1-61194-042-8

Bell Bridge Books is an Imprint of BelleBooks, Inc.

Copyright © 2011 by Sharon Sala

Printed and bound in the United States of America.

We at BelleBooks enjoy hearing from readers.
Visit our websites – www.BelleBooks.com and
www.BellBridgeBooks.com.

10 9 8 7 6 5 4 3 2

Cover design: Debra Dixon
Interior design: Hank Smith
Photo credits:
Girl (manipulated) © Stanislav Perov | Dreamstime.com
Graveyard (manipulated) © Sandra Cunningham | Dreamstime.com

:Llml:01: DS4LSI

For all the girls who are a little bit different—
just know that's what makes you special

And for Chelsea, Logan and Leslie
Now you can finally read my books

Also By Sharon Sala

The Lunatic Detective

CHAPTER ONE

The alarm that Tara Luna had set with such confidence last night yanked her rudely from Channing Tatum's arms, just when he was about to kiss her.

OMG . . . did the universe have a wicked sense of humor or what?

She rolled over to the side of the bed and turned it off.

"What a mood killer," she muttered, and sat up.

She was rubbing sleep out of her eyes when a blob of gray ectoplasm floated from the corner of her room and across her line of vision.

That would be Henry, one of two ghosts who had been with Tara for as long as she could remember. While his presence might seem startling for most teenagers, it wasn't for Tara. She'd always been able to see ghosts. As for Henry, the ghost in question, he'd appeared to her at the age of three, after she'd fallen from a swing and broken her arm, and he hadn't been far from her since. Usually, he appeared to her as a somewhat dim version of what he'd looked like when he'd been alive, like with a head and body—arms—legs—the usual. But when he was irked, which her and Uncle Pat's move from Denver to Oklahoma had caused, he didn't bother. Sometimes this was good. Sometimes it wasn't. Right now, it was disconcerting to strip in front of what had once been a living, breathing male, no matter what gray-blob shape he picked.

"Go away, Henry. I'm about to take a shower."

To show his displeasure, Henry rolled Tara's new ink pen off the edge of her desk onto the floor, then vaporized.

Tara was still muttering beneath her breath as she picked up her pen then headed for the bathroom. Every time she and Uncle Pat moved to a new home, Henry caused trouble. He didn't like disruption anymore than Tara, but at least Henry had an option. Tara didn't. Uncle Pat was all the family she had, and Uncle Pat had a gypsy heart. He was always looking for greener pastures, leaving Tara to say goodbye to old friends and hope that wherever she and Uncle Pat were going, she would find a way to fit in.

She staggered into the bathroom, dropped the t-shirt that she'd slept in, squirted a dollop of shampoo into the palm of her hand, then stepped into the shower. She lifted her face to the water jets, letting the warm water wash away the sleep from her eyes before she started on her hair.

Today was the first day of school and it was also her senior year. They'd moved from Denver, Colorado to Stillwater, Oklahoma less than a week ago, into an old, bungalow-style, white-frame house on Duck Street. The house had been sitting empty for six months, and it had taken a lot of cleaning to make it liveable. But two nights ago, the last box had been unpacked, and as of yesterday afternoon, the windows had curtains. Tomorrow, the television would get hooked up to cable services, the phone would be on, her laptop would be hooked back up to internet services, and life as they knew it would resume.

As she scrubbed at her hair, she thought about the day ahead of her. There was no way it would be good. A new kid— in senior class. How wrong was that? If anyone found out she claimed to be psychic, it would be three strikes and she'd be out before she started.

The shower curtain jiggled. Tara's eyes were shut to keep out the shampoo, but she didn't need to see to know who was causing it. Henry was still acting up.

"If you get water in the floor, I'm not cleaning it up!"

The shower curtain billowed toward her, then plastered the thin plastic sheet to her wet, soapy body.

"Henry! I'm warning you. Back off. Go pester Uncle Pat.

It's *his* fault we moved again, not mine."

At that point, the curtain settled and Tara was able to finish her shower in peace. She could imagine what tricks he was playing on Uncle Pat. She'd be helping her uncle look for his reading glasses or keys before the day was out. Hiding things was one of Henry's best stunts.

She dried and dressed quickly, then took a blow drier to her long dark hair to finish it off. A few minutes later she paused to look at herself in the mirror. On the surface, she didn't appear all that different from any other seventeen-year-old girl. She had an all-right figure, although if she could have picked, she would have opted for legs that weren't so long and gangly. Her face was heart-shaped, like her mother's had been. At least that's what Uncle Pat always said, although Tara wouldn't know.

Other than a photo of them taken at their wedding, she had no memory of either one of her parents. They'd died in a car wreck before her first birthday. Uncle Pat, her mother's brother, was all the family she'd ever known. She realized how amazing it was that a confirmed bachelor with his head in the clouds and his nose always in a book had even bothered with her. But he had. Even when he aggravated her the most, he was still her goofy, loveable Uncle Pat.

She tweezed a wild eyebrow hair, smeared a little mascara on already dark lashes, swiped some lip gloss on her curvy lips, then squinted at the mirror until she could barely see herself. That's when she looked the most like Angelina Jolie, who was her all-time favorite actress. It wasn't about how pretty or famous Angelina was that made Tara like her. It was that she kept adopting kids that no one else wanted.

That, Tara could identify with.

A lock of her hair suddenly floated up. That would be Millicent, the other ghost in the house. Millicent never bothered to materialize past the occasional puff of pink smoke, but Tara could hear her voice, loud and clear, unlike Henry, who never bothered to talk.

I like your hair better up.

3

"I'm leaving it down, thank you," Tara answered, knowing Millicent was just voicing her opinion of Tara's look. Millicent was not shy about speaking her mind or correcting Tara. It never occurred to Tara that the only mother figure she'd ever had was Millicent, the spirit of a woman who'd been dead for over one hundred years.

Tara's life was crazy, but it was all she'd known.

As far as clothes went, her choice and style was straight out of Walmart and Target. Money was always an issue with them, and while she would have loved to wear designer stuff, the truth was, a tee was a tee. Jeans were jeans. Today she was wearing a pink tee and her favorite jeans. They rode low on her hips, while the fabric was soft and old and frayed at the hems—a great grungy look.

It was the best she could do considering half of her clothes were dirty and Uncle Pat had yet to hook up the washer and dryer. She stared at her features, so familiar, yet not what she wished they would be, then made a face at herself and left the bathroom. As she started down the hall, she could already smell the coffee, which meant Uncle Pat had made breakfast. Considering the fact that they'd been unpacking for the better part of three days without taking time to stock the pantry or shop for groceries, she was a little anxious as to what breakfast would be. He had a tendency to cook stuff that was beyond what most people considered a comfort zone.

"Hey, Uncle Pat," Tara said, as she entered the kitchen.

Patrick Carmichael was tall and lean—pushing fifty and beginning to bald. When he was younger, he'd been told he looked a lot like Sean Connery. Tara hadn't known who that was until she'd watched some old James Bond movies. Personally, she hadn't seen the resemblance, but maybe that was because she didn't want to think about her uncle kissing pretty women and taking them to bed like that actor had done. Now, the resemblance to James Bond was long gone, along with his hair.

The fact that Pat's clothes still had the fold marks from packing didn't bother him in the least. When he heard Tara's voice, he turned and waved a spatula at her, then pointed toward the table.

"Good morning, honey," he said. "Breakfast is almost ready."

"Good, I'm hungry," Tara said, as she picked up her juice glass and took a sip. She raised her eyebrows at the taste and then eyed it curiously, wondering what he'd combined to get such an unusual taste.

"How do you like my latest concoction?" he asked.

"It's . . . uh, interesting. What is it?"

"Oh . . . a combination of several things, including orange Gatorade and some melted vanilla ice cream. No sense in wasting good food, right?"

Tara tried to identify another less distinctive flavor. "Did you put some almond flavoring in it, too?"

Pat frowned as he plated their food. "Almond? No, no . . . at least I don't think so." Then he swung toward the table with a plate in each hand. "Here you go! Eat up! You'll need all your energy for your big day."

Tara sighed. He had no idea. She hated always being the new kid in school.

She thrust a fork into what looked like scrambled eggs and took a big bite. It was all she could do not to choke. She managed to swallow without gagging, an eating skill she'd mastered at an early age, and then washed the taste out of her mouth with mystery juice and reached for the plate of toast instead.

Her uncle frowned. "You don't like your food?"

"I don't know if I do or not," Tara said. "What is it?"

Her uncle frowned. "Either you like the taste, or you don't."

She grinned and fired back, "Is it food in its purest form, or is it yet another deadly combination?"

He sighed then poked at his own plate of food. "It's perfectly good squash. I found them growing on some plants in that jungle of a back yard. Thought I'd surprise you."

Tara leaned over and kissed him soundly on the cheek.

"And you did." She reached for the jelly jar then paused. "That is jelly, right?"

He sighed. Obviously his attempt to create a gourmet breakfast had failed. "Yes."

She grinned as she smeared a good helping of jelly on a piece of toast, then took a big bite. "Yum. Grape-a-cot, my favorite."

"There's nothing wrong with mixing grape and apricot jams. They're both fruit. They're both sweet."

"And so are you," Tara said, as she kissed her uncle on the cheek before getting up from the table. "Gotta go. Don't want to be late the first day."

"Don't you want me to drop you off?" he asked.

"No, that's all right, Uncle Pat. Take your time. Eat your breakfast in peace . . . and while you're at it, you can have mine, too."

He grinned wryly. "I'll shop before dinner tonight."

"Get some hamburger meat and I'll cook," she offered, then grabbed her book bag and headed out the door.

"Hey, Tara! Wait a minute!"

Tara turned. "Yeah?"

"My keys. Have you seen my car keys? I can't find them anywhere."

Tara frowned and retraced her steps into the house. "I'll help you look," she said, and when he left the room, she slammed her backpack onto the sofa and put her hands on her hips. "Henry! Cough them up now, and I mean it!" Uncle Pat had no idea about Henry and Millicent. Tara had never had the courage to tell him. He was very skeptical about psychics, ghosts, and anything else that couldn't be explained by logic. She heard a faint jingle coming from down the hall and followed the sound.

"Now, Henry!"

The keys appeared out of nowhere and dropped at her feet.

"Thank you very much," she muttered, then changed the tone of her voice to light and happy. "Hey! Uncle Pat! I found them."

Pat came out of his bedroom. "Great! Where were they?"

"Oh . . . just laying around." She dropped them into his hands. "Have a good day."

"You, too, honey," he said, and kissed the top of her head. She retrieved her backpack and headed out the door. She was halfway down the block, listening to Beyoncé on her iPod, before she realized she was no longer alone. Henry was floating along beside her, obviously in a better mood, and Millicent was absolutely bubbly, chattering in one ear while Tara tried to focus on Beyoncé in the other.

Aren't you excited about starting a new school? There'll be some handsome young men there, I expect.

Tara thought nothing of it. She was used to the company. Henry was bossy, and Millicent was man-crazy. Even if no one else could see them, they were part of her family.

The day started better than Tara expected. She got all the way through first period without anyone paying her much attention. Henry had made himself scarce, and Millicent was probably in the gymnasium, haunting the boys' dressing rooms to sneak a peek. Tara didn't know what kind of life Millicent had lived in the flesh, but as a ghost, she was wicked bad.

It wasn't until second period that Tara got a jolt of reality. She was already in her seat and leafing through her textbook when she realized the room had gotten quiet. She looked up to see what was going on and saw a girl standing by the teacher's desk, glaring at a guy just walking into the room.

The girl gave the boy a drop dead look. The boy didn't even acknowledge her. Tara smiled. You didn't have to be a psychic to figure out they had history. She heard the girl behind her hiss across the aisle.

"SueEllen. SueEllen . . . look! Flynn O'Mara has a tat!"

"Yeah . . . I wonder if his father has one to match."

As soon as Tara looked at the skull-and-barbed-wire tattoo showing beneath the sleeve of Flynn O'Mara's tight t-shirt, she flashed on a jail cell. Bummer. *His Dad's in jail.*

Suddenly Uncle Pat's quirks weren't so bad after all. She dared one more quick look at the tat, but her attention soon moved to the size of the muscle on which it had been inked. Definitely leer-worthy. When he passed beside her on his way toward the back of the room, she caught a whiff of sexy aftershave and stifled a groan. Millicent was going to be all a-twitter over him. Tara just knew it.

When she heard someone behind her whisper, "He's sooo hot," she couldn't help but silently agree.

But it was another girl's answer that made her curious. "Yeah . . . but no one in her right mind would mess with him."

"Bethany did."

"But not for long."

"Yeah. Right."

Ahah. Bethany must be the girl glaring at him beside the teacher's desk.

Then the teacher entered the classroom and Tara's curiosity was left dangling. It was sort of like tuning into the middle of one of Uncle Pat's reality TV shows. Didn't know the characters. Didn't know the plot. Just knew that someone cute was bound to have a bad moment before the hour was up. Something told her that this Flynn guy had already had his bad moment—maybe more than one. But he was definitely cute. And it wasn't a half-bad start to the second hour of the first day of her senior year.

It wasn't until lunch that she was faced with her first test of endurance, and it all began when, trying to maintain a low profile, she sat down at a table in the middle of the school cafeteria.

"Hey. New girl. You can't sit there."

Tara looked up at the blonde who was balancing her tray while glaring at Tara.

"Were you talking to me?" Tara asked.

"Do you see anyone else who looks new?"

Tara grinned. "From where I'm sitting, pretty much everyone."

The blonde rolled her eyes. "These seats are taken."

Tara had spent her life trying to fit in. She thought about just getting up and moving, but it was her senior year, and she was tired of being low-man on the social totem pole.

"Who are you?" Tara asked.

"I'm Prissy."

"I've always admired a girl who can admit to her faults."

The blank look on Prissy's face was all the proof Tara needed to know that the joke had gone right over her head. So she started again.

"Okay, Prissy, why can't I sit here? It's empty."

Prissy rolled her eyes. "You're new, or you wouldn't be so stupid."

"Um . . . actually, I'm not new. I've been around for seventeen years now."

Another zinger that Prissy completely missed.

"Whatever," she drawled. "You still can't sit here. This is the cheerleaders' table."

Tara groaned.

The sound must have carried, because the room went silent. She knew she should just take her tray and move, but she couldn't bring herself to fold at the first challenge. Just once, why couldn't the universe bend to fit *her* world, instead of her always having to bend to fit its?

She stood and jerked the edge of her tray against her belly.

"Cheerleaders," she drawled, and began bowing up and down as she slowly backed away, carrying her tray.

Laughter ricocheted from one end of the lunchroom to the other. Tara lifted her chin and swaggered all the way to the back of the room. When she got to an empty table, she set down her tray then turned and yelled, "Hey Prissy! Prissy!"

Prissy turned, then gaped, unable to believe that the new girl was still trying to communicate with her in any way. Two other girls who'd now joined her at the cheerleaders' table frowned. One of them was Bethany Fanning—the Bethany from second hour who'd had the thing with Mr. Bad Dude Flynn O' Mara. The other was a girl named Melanie Smith, who went by the name of Mel. The trio were all part of Stillwater High's cheerleading squad, and all three were blonde.

"Who's *she?*" Bethany asked.

"I saw her in the hall earlier," Mel added.

Prissy turned bright red as Tara waved at her cheerfully. Tara stopped and pointed to the table where she'd set her tray.

"How about here? Anybody got their name on *this* table?"

Another ripple of giggles rolled across the room.

At the sound of laughter, Prissy's face flushed an even angrier pink. She wasn't used to being laughed at. The other two blondes frowned, but said nothing.

Tara sat down and made a big production of setting her silverware in the proper place, opening her milk carton and inserting a straw, then salting and peppering everything on her plate before she began to eat. She was chewing her first bite when she happened to look up and catch Flynn grinning at her.

She smiled back, only afterward realizing that she'd been chewing salad when she smiled. She sighed, hoping nothing green had been sticking out from between her teeth, and finished her meal in silence.

As she'd feared, her transition into the new school was off to an awkward and uncomfortable start. What she hadn't expected was for Millicent to intervene next.

Tara was on her way out of the lunchroom when she heard a loud shriek. She turned just in time to see Prissy's plate of food levitate from the table and fly into her lap.

"Way to go, Millicent." Tara kept on walking.

She heading for her locker when some guy behind her called out, "Hey! Hey! Wait up!"

Surely he's not talking to me, she thought, and kept on walking. Suddenly the guy grabbed her by the arm. She spun, ready to do battle. *OMG, it's the hottie.*

"Hey," Flynn said, and quickly turned her loose. "I'm Flynn. You're new, right?"

"Only to this school. Not to the world."

He grinned. "Got a name to go with that mouth?"

"Tara Luna."

His smile was hypnotizing. "Luna. That means moon, right?"

Her brain stopped working. She gazed up at him silently.

Talk to him, Tara. Say something witty. Say anything.

Tara sighed. Millicent. She should have known she'd get involved in this.

"So I'm told," she said, then stifled the urge to roll her eyes. *Could my answer have gotten any dumber?*

"Moon girl. That's not half bad."

The bell rang, breaking up what might have been the defining moment of the day for Tara. Instead of an undying declaration of love, he gave her forearm a soft jab with his fist.

"See ya, moon girl."

Tara was still trying to come up with a real cute way to say goodbye when he disappeared into the room across the hall.

Way to miss the opportunity of the day.

Can it, Millicent. Don't you have someplace to be? Some half-naked jock to ogle?

Millicent laughed and went silent.

When the last bell rang, Tara was exhausted, both mentally and physically. She'd gotten lost trying to find her fourth-period classroom, and arrived to find Flynn the Hottie was in that class, as well. The fact that he kept looking at her with more than curiosity made her nervous. She thought she might like him—really like him—but she was cautious. The last thing she needed was to fall for someone again. Before the move from Denver, she'd had her first serious boyfriend. Millicent had gone along on every one of their dates, suddenly determined to play chaperone. Uncle Pat's decision to move came just as the relationship was heating up

Tara sagged. Why bother falling for another guy? It would hurt too much when Uncle Pat pulled up stakes again.

My life sucks, she thought.

There was nothing to do but go home and hope tomorrow was a better day.

That evening, Tara was taking a meatloaf out of the oven when she heard the front door open. Uncle Pat was home.

"Just in time," she called out, then set the hot dish on a trivet and gave the green beans a quick stir.

When her uncle didn't answer, she decided he hadn't heard her and she wiped her hands on a dish towel then went to the living room to greet him. But there was no one there.

"Uncle Pat?"

She glanced toward the hallway leading to their bedrooms, then went in search of him before their food got cold. She knocked on his bedroom door, then opened it for a peek. He wasn't there.

"This is so weird," she muttered. She knocked at the door to the hall bath. No Uncle Pat. "Okay. I heard the door open and close. So maybe he didn't come in. Maybe he stepped back outside to get something from the car."

She hurried back into the living room, but when she looked out, the car wasn't in the driveway.

"Okay. This isn't funny! Henry! Was that you?"

Henry appeared in the far corner of the room. "Not I," he said. "Millicent, did you open the door?"

No. Doors are so trite. Any ghost can do doors.

"Well, excuse me." She looked around one last time then shrugged and started toward the kitchen. Suddenly a dark shadow appeared in the doorway, blocking her path. She froze.

This couldn't be good.

The shadow came toward her, then *through* her, leaving her so cold she couldn't move and so shocked she couldn't speak. *That was beyond rude.* A kind of ghostly slap in the face.

"Something smells good! I'm starving!"

Uncle Pat's voice shattered Tara's focus. She shivered, then turned. The shadow was gone. It was only Uncle Pat in his flower power t-shirt and old bell-bottom pants coming in the front door. It was hard to say which was freakier—the ghost that had passed through her or Uncle Pat's crazy clothes.

"It's meatloaf," she said, and then swiped her hands across her face and headed back to the kitchen to finish up the meal.

It wasn't the first time she'd been confronted by a dark spirit, and it probably wouldn't be the last, but she absolutely hated it.

"Let me wash up and I'll help you," Uncle Pat said, and hurried down the hall.

Tara was dishing up green beans when he came back into the kitchen.

"How was school?"

She rolled her eyes. "Where do I start? Let's see . . . I chose the wrong place to sit in the lunchroom. I got lost on the way to gym class, and there's a cute guy named Flynn in two of my classes, with what might be some kind of prison tattoo on his arm."

Pat frowned. "I'm not liking this Flynn guy."

Tara sighed. "Don't worry. He barely noticed me."

"You do remember my lecture about sex, right? I mean . . . I'm not advocating you have sex , but I do not want you unprepared, either. If you want, I'll take you to a doctor and—"

"Uncle Pat! Trust me, I'm not going to have sex with a guy I just met today. I am not stupid, okay?"

Her uncle's frown deepened.

"All right, but be careful." He poked at the meatloaf. "This looks good. Did you put some hot peppers in it?"

"No."

"Oh. I was hoping for some jalapenos at least. Why not?"

"Because you didn't buy any."

"Oh. Right. I'll add it to the next grocery list. For now, let's eat. I'm starved."

Thankful that their conversation had taken a less embarrassing turn, Tara finished dishing up the food, filled their glasses with iced tea, and then joined her uncle at the table and handed him her plate. He loaded it with a thick slab of meatloaf. Tara added a spoonful of green beans, a helping of mashed potatoes, and then reached for the ketchup. Hamburger in any form was always better with ketchup and anything was better than her Uncle Pat launching into one of his attempts at parental advice.

Chapter Two

Four days later, the dark shadow came back.

It was three minutes after four in the morning when Tara woke up needing to go to the bathroom. She was on her way back to bed when she sensed she was no longer alone. Her heart skipped a beat as the darkness between her and the hallway moved into her room. A normal girl's first instinct would have been to scream or run away, but Tara was used to spooks. She stomped into her bedroom with her hand in the air.

"Look, Smokey . . . I'm bordering on PMS, so you don't want to mess with me. State your business or make yourself scarce. And don't go *through* me again to do it. I'll tell Henry and Millicent to kick your behind so hard you'll never be able to put two ectoplasmic molecules together again. Do you read me?"

The shadow shifted then disappeared through the floor.

"That's better," Tara muttered, then headed to the dresser, where she'd left her jewelry box. She dug through it until she found her Saint Benedict's medal, fastened the chain around her neck, and then crawled back into bed. "Like I don't already have enough to deal with," she said wearily, then punched her pillow a couple of times before settling back to sleep.

All too soon, the alarm was going off and another strange day was in motion.

The first week at school sped by without further trouble. At home, Uncle Pat got cable hooked up to the TV and internet to Tara's laptop. She caught up on episodes of *Glee* and *Gossip Girl*. She was beginning to believe everything was smoothing out. Then week two came, reminding her she was still the new kid in school.

Tara was on her way to first period when she turned a corner in the hall and came up on the cheerleader trio who she now thought of as The Blonde Mafia. Prissy saw Tara, then pointed at her and said something that sent the other two into a fit of giggles.

"You are so lame. You're almost as funny as your name," Prissy said, as Tara walked past.

Tara rolled her eyes. "Is that rhyme supposed to pass for white girl rap?"

Prissy's face flushed angrily as kids standing nearby heard it go down and started laughing, but Tara didn't hang around for a second stanza. She didn't have time for their petty crap. She walked about ten feet further down the hall when she heard a shriek and turned just in time to see two hanks of Prissy's hair suddenly standing straight up on either side of her face like donkey ears.

Millicent! Tara stifled a grin. "I knew that was gonna happen," she said, and kept on walking.

Tara's first-period teacher was at her desk, poking frantically at the screen of her smart phone. She looked up when Tara walked in, nodded distractedly, then returned to what she'd been doing. The air was so thick with distress that Tara immediately sensed what was wrong.

Mrs. Farmer had money troubles.

That was something she understood. She and Uncle Pat rarely had an excess of the green stuff, themselves. And considering that his new job with the city of Stillwater involved reading electric meters, they weren't going to get rich this year, either.

She slipped into her seat, then took her book out of her backpack, trying to concentrate on something besides the misery Mrs. Farmer was projecting. But for a psychic, it was like trying to ignore the water while going through a car wash. Tara was inundated with wave after wave of her teacher's thoughts and emotions.

All of a sudden she knew Mrs. Farmer's husband drank too much. Her mother was a nag. Her sister was married to a doctor, which made her own husband's problems seem even worse. And suddenly Tara knew something Mrs. Farmer did not.

It wasn't that Mrs. Farmer couldn't manage her money. *Someone was stealing it.*

The room began to fill with other students, and a few minutes later the bell rang, signaling the beginning of class. Tara felt Mrs. Farmer trying to focus on her job and Tara tried to do the same. English was one of her favorite classes.

"Good morning," Mrs. Farmer said. "Your assignment over the weekend was to read the poem, *The Female of the Species,* by Rudyard Kipling, then write a one-hundred word paper on it. This morning we're going to read your papers aloud in class."

The collective groan that followed her announcement was no surprise. Tara sensed that half the class hadn't even read the poem and of the ones who had, less than a dozen had completed the assignment. Tara pulled out her notes but had a difficult time focusing. She kept keying in on Mrs. Farmer's plight.

She knew what needed to be done to help her, but it meant making herself vulnerable.

The hour passed, and when the bell rang students scattered, even as Mrs. Farmer was still giving them their assignment for tomorrow. Tara had argued with herself all through class, when she really hadn't had an option. If she'd seen someone stealing, she would have told. Knowing it was happening and who was doing it and not telling was the same thing to her. She waited until the last of the students were gone, then headed toward the front of the room, where her teacher was erasing the blackboard.

"Mrs. Farmer, may I speak with you a minute?"

Unaware anyone had lingered behind, Mrs. Farmer whirled around, startled. "Oh, my. You startled me, dear. I didn't know anyone was still here. You're Tara, right?"

"Yes, ma'am." Tara sighed. There was nothing to do but jump in with both feet. "I need to ask you something, and then I need to *tell* you something."

She could see the confusion on her teacher's face, but she had to hurry or she'd be late for second period.

"Who's Carla?" Tara asked.

"Why . . . that's my babysitter," Mrs. Farmer said. "She stays at my home during the day and takes care of my twin daughters. They're only three."

"Okay . . . I need to tell you that she's stealing money from you. She's taking blank checks out of the new pads of checks in the box and forging your signature. That's why you're account stays overdrawn."

Tara could see all the color fade from her teacher's face. Mrs. Farmer gasped. "How do you know this?"

Tara sighed. "I just do, okay?"

Mrs. Farmer grabbed her by the arm. "Do you know Carla Holloway? Did she *tell* you this?"

"No, ma'am. I asked you who Carla is, remember? Uncle Pat and I just moved here, remember? We really don't know anyone."

"Then how . . . "

"Maybe I'm psychic, okay? When you go home this evening, get out your new checks and look through the pads. You'll find a couple of checks will be missing from each one. Confront Carla. She'll fold. And don't forgive her to the point of letting her keep babysitting for you . . . because she's using the money to buy drugs."

"Oh dear Lord," Mrs. Farmer gasped, and reached for her cell phone.

Tara ducked her head and made a run for the hall. She'd done all she could do. The rest was up to Mrs. Farmer.

She made it to second period just as the last bell rang. That teacher frowned as she slid into her seat. Tara heard a soft masculine whisper from behind her.

"Good save, Moon girl."

She turned. Flynn O'Mara grinned at her. Tara rolled her

eyes and then dug her book out of her backpack, trying not to think about how stinkin' cute Flynn was. Kind of had that classic heartthrob look, but with more muscles and straighter hair.

Henry showed up about fifteen minutes later and began trying to get Tara's attention. She sent him mental signals to be quiet, but he wasn't getting the message. Just before class ended they heard a loud commotion out in the hall. It sounded like doors banging—dozens of doors—against the walls. Henry threw up his hands and vaporized. That's when she realized whatever was going on out in the hall might have something to do with Millicent. The door to her classroom opened and flew back against the wall with a loud bang. The fact that it seemed to have opened by itself was not lost on the teacher or the students.

"Wait here!" the teacher cried, and dashed out into the hall.

Moments later Tara heard the fire alarm go off. The teacher came running back into the room.

"Walk in an orderly line and follow me!" Students grabbed backpacks and folders and fell into line behind her as she strode quickly out the door.

Tara's stomach sank as she slid in between Flynn O'Mara and a girl with blue hair.

"It's probably nothing," Flynn said over her shoulder.

Tara shivered. She knew better. It was something all right. It was Millicent. But why?

The halls grew crowded as students filed out of the classroom and made for the exits. To their credit, the exodus was somewhat orderly. As soon as they reached the school grounds, security guards began directing them to the appropriate areas. In the distance, Tara could hear sirens.

She kept looking back toward the school building. What had Millicent done?

Henry appeared in front of her, as if to say *I told you so*, then disappeared just as quickly again. A pair of fire trucks pulled into the school yard. Firemen jumped down from the rigs and hurried into the building. As Tara watched, smoke began to pour out of one of the windows on the second floor.

OMG! Millicent had set the school on fire? Why would Tara's lifelong ghost pal set the school on fire?

The moment she thought it, Tara heard Millicent's voice in her head.

I didn't set the fire. It was already burning between the walls. Give me a break. I was trying to help.

Sorry, Tara told her.

As if that wasn't enough drama for the day, a loud rumble of thunder suddenly sounded overhead.

Ghosts couldn't control the weather, so this wasn't Henry or Millicent's doing. A strong gust of wind suddenly funneled between the school and the gym. She shuddered. Even though the day was warm, that wind gust was chilly. Then it thundered again. She looked up at the underside of the building storm clouds, frowning at how dark they were getting.

"Are you cold?" Flynn asked.

She turned to find him standing right behind her.

"A little. Who knew we'd need jackets today? It was in the nineties when I left home this morning."

"Take mine," he said, as he slipped out of his denim jacket and then put it over her shoulders.

"Then you'll be cold," she said.

"Nah. I'm good."

She slipped the jacket on. The warmth from his body still lingered in the fabric, giving her a momentary impression of how it would feel to have his arms around her. It was an image that made her blush.

The wind continued to rise, with thunder rumbling every few minutes.

Tara shivered nervously as she looked up at the clouds. She hated storms.

"We're going to get soaked," she muttered.

A shaft of lightning suddenly snaked out of the clouds and struck nearby, sending the crowd into a panic.

"Into the gym!" Coach Jones yelled.

He waved his arms and pushed kids toward the gym.

"To the gymnasium!" a teacher echoed, and the crowd began to move. When the next shaft of lightning struck, this time in the football field nearby, they began to run. And then the rain came down.

Tara ran as hard as everyone else, but the ground was getting muddy and more than once she lost traction and slipped. If she fell, she would get trampled before anyone knew she was even down there. No sooner had the thought gone through her mind than her feet went out from under her. She was falling and all she could see were the legs of hundreds of students aiming straight for her.

Suddenly, Flynn pulled her upright. "Hang on to me, Moon Girl!"

She grabbed hold of his hand. Together they made it into the gym. They were heading for the bleachers before they realized they were still holding hands. They turned loose of each other too quickly, then grinned for being so silly.

"Thanks for your help," she said, and took off his jacket. "It's soaked. Sorry."

"It'll dry. Are you okay?"

"Yeah. Sure. Thanks again."

He eyed the dark hair plastered to her head and the wet t-shirt she was wearing as his grin widened. "You might wanna keep that jacket for a while." She looked down, then rolled her eyes. Everything—and she did mean, everything—showed, right down to her blue bra and the little mole next to her belly button.

"Perfect," Tara muttered. "Just perfect."

"Yeah. I agree," Flynn said.

She thumped him on the arm and then crossed her arms across her chest.

"Stop looking," she hissed.

"I'm trying, but hey . . . don't blame me for an appreciation of the finer things in life."

Tara laughed despite herself, then put his jacket back on and climbed the bleachers. She sat down a little away from a crowd of sophomores and began wringing the water out of her hair.

I like her, Flynn thought. *I like this crazy girl.*

Flynn paused. If he followed her up and sat down beside her, it would only intensify what he was already feeling. There was no pretense with her. She was a little odd and definitely different from the other girls in school, but he had plans for his last year of high school that didn't include getting messed up by another female. Bethany Fanning had done it to him big time over the summer, and he wasn't in the mood to go through another dose of female drama. Still, something told him that Tara Luna wasn't fake, and if there *was* drama in her life, she wasn't the kind to exaggerate it.

He felt someone push him toward her, but when he turned around, there was no one there. Frowning, he climbed the bleachers and then plopped down right in front of her. That way he was close, but not staking out territory.

Tara had seen Millicent give Flynn a push. So, Millicent wasn't satisfied with playing havoc at school today. Now she was playing matchmaker.

I delivered him. You do the rest.

"I can do just fine on my own, thank you," Tara said beneath her breath.

Flynn frowned. "Sorry. I didn't know you'd set up boundaries. Want me to move?"

"No. No. Not you. I wasn't talking to you. Sit here . . . wherever you want. Sorry."

Flynn's frown deepened as he looked around. "Then who were you talking to, if not to me?"

"Ghosts," Tara said. "I was talking to ghosts."

"Yeah, right. Whatever. I can take a hint." He got up and moved away.

Now see what you did.

"Just stop meddling," Tara snapped.

Whatever, Millicent said, echoing Flynn, then made herself scarce.

Tara slumped. Could this day possibly get any worse?

About an hour later, the school principal came into the gym and made an announcement. The fire department had put out the blaze, but the students would not be allowed back into the building until they were sure it was safe. So, as soon as the storm passed, high school would be dismissed and the students were to go home. The principal also announced that anyone who was carrying a cell phone was allowed to use it to call home. Normally, kids had to keep them turned off.

Tara had a phone but, knowing there was no one home to call, she didn't bother. As she walked out of the building she looked around for Flynn to give him back his jacket, but he was gone.

"Great. Just freakin' great," she muttered, as she headed down the sidewalk. She'd definitely messed up with the only guy who'd been nice to her.

The closer she got to home, she began to forget about him. There was an uneasy feeling in the pit of her stomach, like someone had just died. Something told her it had to do with that dark spirit.

Uncle Pat would be at work, which meant she'd be home alone for at least four or five hours. Plenty of time for the dark entity to plague her some more. If only she could figure it out. She couldn't tell if it was threatening her, or just an unhappy spirit. Either way, it was the last thing she was in the mood to face. She fingered the chain around her neck, then followed it all the way down to the medallion with the image of St. Benedict on one side, and his prayer for protection on the other.

"I'm needing all the help I can get here, please."

Henry popped up beside her. She smiled.

"Thanks, Henry. You are so my BFF."

What about me?

"You, too, Millicent. What does this say about me . . . claiming two ghosts as BFFs?"

A soft wind began to encircle her—the ghost version of a hug. She would have cried if it would have done any good.

"Thanks," she said, and then added. "So, guys, I need a

big favor. See what you can find out about Shadow Guy. Why is he hanging around me, and even more to the point . . . is he evil?"

At that point her cell phone rang. She didn't need to look at Caller ID to see who it was. Uncle Pat was the only live soul in the listings. That didn't preclude the occasional weird text messages she got from Millicent and Henry, but when they wanted her attention, they never rang the phone.

"Hi Uncle Pat, what's up?"

"Are you okay?" he asked. "We heard at work that there was a fire in the high school."

"Oh. Shoot. I should have called to at least tell you that," she said. "Yes, I'm fine, but class was dismissed for the day. In fact, I'm on my way home right now. The firemen wanted to do a thorough sweep before letting us back into classes."

"What was burning?" he asked.

"Not sure. Probably electrical. I heard it started behind a wall." She didn't bother to explain that she'd heard it from Millicent. Uncle Pat tolerated just about everything she did except her claim to see ghosts. She'd learned a long time ago to keep all that to herself.

"Well, thank goodness you're all right," he said. "So, you'll be okay at home alone?"

She thought about the dark entity, then sighed. Even if she told him, and even if he believed her, there was nothing he could do.

"I'll be fine. And since I'll have lots of time, I'll make something special for supper tonight, okay?"

"There are some bratwursts in the freezer."

"Yum," she said, thankful he couldn't see her face. Uncle Pat's idea of a culinary delight was brats and beer. "So quit worrying about me. I'll be fine."

"Okay then. See you later alligator." Glad there was no one around to hear, she fired back with a response he'd taught her when she was barely old enough to talk. "After while, crocodile."

"Peace out," he replied.

She was still smiling when she heard him disconnect. Uncle Pat was such an old hippie. She dropped the phone back into her book bag and kept on walking. A few moments later she heard a siren in the distance, and turned to see if she could tell what was going on. To her dismay, she could see a new plume of smoke. The fire must have restarted in the high school. She was beginning to wonder if there would be a school to go back to, when she saw a red convertible turn a corner a few blocks up, then head her way.

She'd seen it in the school parking lot and knew it belonged to a boy named Davis Breedlove. She also knew he was the star quarterback for the football team and that he and Bethany Fanning had a thing going on, which meant her blonde entourage would probably be along for the ride. Telling herself not to borrow trouble, she turned around and kept walking, hoping they'd ignore her as they drove past. When she heard the car slowing down, then shouts and laughter, she sighed. She'd bet a new Blackberry it was that goofy twitch, Prissy.

"Hey, hey, it's the new funny girl. Hey Tara Luna . . . or is your name *Lunatic*? Tara Lunatic? Are you a lunatic?"

"If this keeps up much longer I will be," Tara mumbled to herself and kept on walking.

"Where'd you get Flynn O'Mara's jacket, lunatic? That's quick work. Already putting out. That's the only way you'd get a hottie's jacket, even if he *is* a bad boy hottie."

Tara stopped and turned. She'd been right about who was driving the car. Davis Breedlove. And Bethany, the girl who'd given Flynn the evil eye the first day of school, was sitting beside him. But it was Prissy the twitch who kept mouthing off. Obviously, her part in the entourage was that of court jester.

Tara knew she should just ignore them, but she was really tired of this crap. She sauntered over to the car, then leaned against it to visit, as if they were her best friends.

"Nice car," she drawled, and smiled at Davis Breedlove. A little taken aback by her nerve, he smiled back.

Bethany bristled. The nobody had just flirted with her boyfriend. That was so not cool.

Prissy caught the look on Bethany's face and did what she did best—she attacked.

"Back off, bitch."

Tara smiled again, this time at Prissy, but it was not friendly.

"You're saving money to get a boob job and your Dad watches porno on the web."

Prissy's mouth was open, but nothing was coming out. The shock on her face was obvious.

Then Tara pointed at Melanie Smith, the other girl in the backseat beside Prissy.

"You binge and purge. Bad habit. I'd give it a rest before all your teeth rot and fall out."

"Oh my God," Mel whimpered, and covered her face with her hands.

A guilty pang made Tara back away from poor Mel. Tara pointed at Bethany, then stopped as something sinister slid through her mind. She didn't know what it was, but something bad was going to happen to Bethany—and soon.

"You need to be careful about who you hang out with."

Davis revved the engine. "Are you dissing me?"

Tara stepped back just in time to keep the car from rolling over her toes, then watched until it disappeared around a curve. She couldn't quit thinking about Bethany's aura of trouble. Maybe she should have said more to warn her. Tara gave a tired shrug. *Who'd believe me?* She shifted her backpack to a more comfortable position and picked up her pace. The sooner she got home, the happier she'd be.

Or so she thought, right up until the moment she stepped up on the porch. Before she knew what was happening, she was surrounded in darkness. A horrible pressure pushed through her mind, followed by a sudden bout of nausea so intense she almost gagged. The cross on the chain around her neck began to burn against her skin. She wanted to scream, but nothing came out. One minute her hand was on the doorknob and then the world began to spin.

Help me, she thought, and then everything went black.

"Tara! Moon girl! Are you all right?"

Tara groaned. She could hear someone calling her name, but she couldn't focus.

Flynn was in a panic. He'd followed her home to apologize for acting like a jerk in the gym. He'd been several blocks behind her on Duck Street when he'd seen Davis Breedlove's car pull over to the curb. He'd seen Tara talking to Bethany and her crew, and he felt sure they were taunting her. It's what people like them did. When they'd finally driven away, he began walking faster, hoping to catch up with Tara, only she'd reached her house first.

He'd seen her step up on the porch and then stagger. She'd had her hand on the doorknob and then all of a sudden she was down. He'd sprinted the last half a block.

"Tara . . . " Suddenly she could breathe. Whatever had attacked her was gone. She grabbed onto the only steady thing she could feel, unaware it was Flynn O'Mara's arm.

"I've got you," Flynn said. "Take it easy. Don't sit up too fast."

Tara shivered, then opened her eyes. "Flynn?"

He breathed a sigh of relief. "Yeah, Moon girl, it's me. Are you okay? Do you hurt anywhere?"

"I am so screwed," Tara mumbled.

"I didn't do it," Flynn said.

Tara scrubbed her hands across her face. "I didn't mean you," she said. "Help me up, will you?"

"Are you sure you're okay to stand up?"

Tara grimaced. She was fine. Now. Unless Creepy came back, she'd still be fine.

"Yes. I'm sure. I can't believe that just happened."

Flynn helped her to her feet. "Did you get dizzy? Did you hit your head when you fell?" He kept running his fingers all over her head, trying to make sure she wasn't bleeding anywhere.

"I don't know," she said. "One minute I was up, then I was down. My key is in my jeans pocket. Wait while I . . . "

Flynn thrust his hand into her pocket, felt the key ring, and pulled it out before she could argue. He unlocked the door, then helped her walk into the living room. He guided her to the sofa. She sank down on it with a thump, and then leaned back and closed her eyes.

"Do you want me to call your parents? Does your mom work somewhere?"

"I don't have a mom. I don't have parents. Just Uncle Pat."

Flynn looked shocked. He'd thought he had it bad—his dad was in prison and his mom worked so many jobs they rarely saw each other. And yet he had parents, which was way more than Tara could claim.

"Sorry. I didn't know," he said.

Tara wanted to do was crawl under the couch and never come out again.

"It's okay," she said, and then felt tears on her cheeks. "Crap. I never cry." She swiped at her face.

"Come here," he said softly, and took her in his arms and gave her a hug.

Tara was too rattled to pull back, and too weak to hide how she felt. Before she knew it, she was sobbing.

"What did they say to you?" he asked.

"They who?" Tara asked, then pulled a tissue out of the box on the lamp table, wiped her eyes and blew her nose.

"I saw Breedlove stop. Bethany, Prissy, and Mel can be real twits. What did they say to you?"

That was when Tara realized he thought she was crying because of the confrontation. If he really knew . . .

"That's not . . . they didn't . . . " she sighed. "Let it go, Flynn. I got dizzy. I'm okay now." Then she caught his hand and threaded her fingers through it. "Thank you . . . again. You keep coming to my rescue."

Flynn wanted to kiss her. He wanted to kiss her real bad

but he wasn't a player He figured that would be a scummy thing to do, considering she was having a weak moment.

"It's my pleasure, Moon girl," he said, gave her fingers a gentle squeeze, then touched his forehead to hers briefly before pulling away.

"I think I'd better lay down for a while," Tara said.

Flynn stood abruptly. "Yeah. Sure. If you're sure you don't need something . . ."

"I'm good," Tara said.

"Yeah, and I'm a monkey's uncle." Tara's eyes widened, then she smiled—slowly—but it was a smile.

"My Uncle Pat is always saying that, too."

Flynn shrugged and grinned. "It's old school, yeah. Something my dad used to say." Then he paled, as he realized he'd just brought up the subject he most hated to address.

"Uncle Pat's favorite thing is 'See you later, alligator.' I'm supposed to answer with, 'After while, crocodile'."

Flynn was so relieved she hadn't questioned him about his dad that he laughed out loud.

Tara knew what he was thinking. She felt his shame and embarrassment and also the frustration at a situation he couldn't control. But she wasn't about to tell him.

"You're sure you gonna be okay if I leave?" Flynn repeated.

"I'm sure," Tara said, even though she wasn't sure of anything anymore.

"Then, I guess I'll be going."

Tara knew he wanted to kiss her. She could feel every crazy thought that was running through his mind—even the stuff that made her blush.

"Oh . . .I'll wash your jacket and bring it to you tomorrow, okay?"

"Yeah, sure," Flynn said, and headed for the door with Tara following so she could lock the door behind him.

Flynn got all the way to the door before he paused and turned.

"Well, hell," he muttered, then gave Tara what was

supposed to be a quick kiss. But it turned into something longer—lingering—sweet and tempting.

"I'm not going to say I'm sorry," he said, when they finally stopped.

Tara felt herself smiling like a lovesick fool.

"You better not," she said, then watched him leave.

Chapter Three

Henry and Millicent were sitting at the foot of Tara's bed when she got to her room.

"Where were you two when I needed you?" Tara asked, as she began digging through the dresser and closets for every religious icon she could find.

Oddly, they had nothing to say to her, and she didn't have time to delve into why they were suddenly so silent.

She pulled out a Bible, a china figurine of an angel, and a small, framed photo of *The Last Supper* that Uncle Pat insisted on packing each time they moved, although she couldn't remember the last time he'd hung it on a wall.

Then she wandered into the kitchen, grabbed the container of salt and headed outside. Without missing a beat, she began pouring a ring of salt all the way around their little house, even wading through knee-high weeds in the back yard to do it. When she was done, she stomped back inside and dug through the kitchen spices until she found a small shaker of dried sage. It wasn't exactly what she needed, but it was going to have to serve. She poured the dried herbs into a shallow bowl, set it on fire then blew it out, leaving nothing but a mini-smudge pot smoking in the bowl. Carrying it with her, she began to move from room to room, saying a cleansing prayer and waving the smoking sage through the air as she went. Once she was done with that, she cleaned up the mess, washed the bowl, and put it back in the cabinet. She'd already had the day from hell. Coming up with a reason for Uncle Pat as to why there was suddenly no salt in the house and why the rooms smelled like burnt salad dressing was going to be tricky enough without leaving the evidence out for him to see.

Satisfied that she'd done all she knew how to do, she put

the Bible under her pillow, the china angel on the table beside her bed, set the small copy of *The Last Supper* on her dresser, and then crawled into bed. She pulled the covers up around her ears and fell asleep clutching her St. Benedict's medal, while Henry and Millicent, well aware they'd faltered seriously in protecting her, stood watch over her bed.

Tara didn't wake up until her bed started shaking. On the verge of a scream, she came to enough to realize it was only Uncle Pat leaning over the bed, giving her shoulder a gentle shake.

"Honey, are you sick?" he asked.

Tara groaned, threw the covers off, and sat up on the side of the bed.

"No. Not really. What time is it?" She looked toward the windows.

"It's after six. I just got home. The house smells funny. Didn't expect to find you in bed."

The sage, she thought. "Oh. Yeah. We need to put air fresheners on the grocery list. The house smelled a little bit like skunk when I got home so I burned a little sage in the rooms, hoping to get rid of it."

"Oh. Well. My goodness. I suppose I need to get that back yard cleaned up and mowed. Too many places for varmints like that to hide. I'll get it done this coming Saturday."

"I'll see about supper," Tara offered.

"Don't worry," Uncle Pat said. "We'll go out instead. There's a neat place not far from here called Eskimo Joe's. It's sort of a burger joint, but with a lot of other options. Nothing fancy, but the food is real good."

"Sounds great," Tara said, and meant it. Eating brats for supper had not been high on her list of favorite foods. "Just give me a couple of minutes."

"Sure, sure. I need to change clothes, anyway. Take your time." He got all the way to the doorway before he stopped and looked back. "Are you sure you're okay? I mean . . . you never sleep in the middle of the day. Is it your period or—"

Tara rolled her eyes. "Uncle Pat! This is so not a topic for discussion, okay?"

He looked a little embarrassed, then shrugged. "Okay. Okay."

Thirty minutes later they were sliding into an empty booth near the back of Eskimo Joe's. Judging by the line out front, the people shopping in the attached gift shop, and the number of patrons already seated at the tables, Uncle Pat's opinion of Joe's food was shared by a good many others.

A slim, middle-aged woman with pretty eyes and brown hair served glasses of water with the menus she left on the table.

"I'll give you a little time to look over the menus and be right back to take your orders, okay?"

"Yeah, sure, Mona," Uncle Pat said, and then frowned when Tara's eyebrows rose.

"You know her name?" Tara asked, as the waitress moved away.

He made a big deal of opening the menu. "She was our waitress at noon, today. One of the guys I work with knows her. Said she has a son in high school and her ex is in prison somewhere for burglary."

Tara tried not to be shocked, but she suddenly realized she'd just met Flynn O'Mara's mother. She glanced through the menu, her mind churning.

"I think I'm gonna order chicken strips," Tara said.

Thankful the subject was changed, her uncle slid into a quick conversation about how his mother used to make fried chicken on Sunday for everyone, and how his sister, Shelly, who was Tara's mother, always got one of the drumsticks because she was the baby.

Since Tara never tired of hearing about the life of a mother she couldn't remember, she urged him to continue. They were still talking about her when Mona came back and took their orders. When their food arrived, Tara made a point of really looking at the waitress serving their food, and saw the resemblance to Flynn.

"Thank you," she said, as Mona put her plate of food in front of her. "It looks good."

Mona didn't bother to hide her surprise. Most of the high school kids she served didn't acknowledge her or the services she provided them. She smiled.

"You're welcome," she said. "I'll be back around with refills for your drinks in a few. Enjoy!"

They were almost through with their meal when Tara suddenly picked up on a bad vibe. The strength of it was frightening. She looked up, casually scanning the diners as if looking for Mona, but in reality she was trying to figure out whose thoughts she'd picked up on.

Then her focus centered on two men standing near the door. She knew within seconds of looking at the taller one's face that he had a gun in his pocket, and she knew the shorter, older one was high on something. His jittery, disconnected thoughts ricocheted through her head so fast it gave her a headache.

They were planning a robbery.

But not here. Sometime before midnight they were going to break into and rob a jewelry store. The name *Beckman's Jewelry*, then *Main Street* slid through her mind so fast she almost missed it. She looked away, and reached for the salt shaker but her fingers were trembling as she shook it over her plate. She had to do something, but she wasn't quite sure what.

Call the police, silly.

The sound of Millicent's voice was definitely welcome. And Millicent was right. All she had to do was phone in what she'd "overheard." The police didn't have to know that she hadn't *really* heard them say anything out loud. Only . . . she didn't want the police to be able to trace the call to her. When it came to being psychic, it was important to stay out of the limelight.

"Uncle Pat, do you know where the restrooms are?"

He looked up, then pointed to the right corner of the dining room. "Somewhere over that way."

"Okay, thanks. I'll be right back."

"Um . . . do you want any dessert?" he asked.

"None for me. You have some though, if you want. I don't have much homework, so there's no need to rush."

He looked pleased at her suggestion and was already scanning the menu when Tara walked away.

She looked for a pay phone all the way through the restaurant, then finally spied one.

She glanced over her shoulder. Uncle Pat was talking to Mona again, supposedly ordering dessert. But she suspected Uncle Pat was somewhat taken with Flynn O'Mara's mother. He probably freak if he knew the boy who'd caught her eye was Mona's son. She made a quick grab for the phone, slid some coins into the slot, then quickly dialed 911.

There were people standing all around her, waiting to be seated, so she turned her back to the crowd and lowered her voice so she wouldn't be overheard.

"911," the dispatcher said. "What's your emergency?"

"Um . . . I just overheard a conversation between two men who are planning a robbery tonight. I heard them say Beckman's Jewelry."

"May I have your name?" the dispatcher asked.

"I don't want anyone to know I overheard. It's not healthy to be a snitch."

She hung up the phone and hurried back to her Uncle Pat. Luckily, he was watching Mona and didn't notice she was coming back from a different direction. She slid into her chair with a breezy smile.

"Let me guess. You ordered lemon meringue pie, didn't you?" she asked.

Her uncle grinned. "You know me, don't you, kiddo?"

A sharp tug of love for her goofy uncle shot through her so fast it brought tears to her eyes.

"Yeah, I guess I do," Tara said, and then took a quick drink of her iced tea.

At that moment, Mona returned with his pie. "You didn't want anything, honey?" she asked, as she looked at Tara.

"No, ma'am. I'm fine."

The big smile Mona gave her made her feel good, even if she wasn't sure why. It was nice to be appreciated for a change.

A few moments later, she happened to look up just as Flynn walked in. She flashed on that goodbye kiss he'd given her earlier today and felt her face getting hot. When he began looking around the restaurant, she realized he was looking for his mom.

When he saw her coming out of the kitchen carrying an order, his face lit up as he grinned and waved.

That's cool, Tara thought.

She continued to sneak looks at him, watching as he stood aside while Mona served the food she was carrying. A few moments later, as they greeted each other with a hug and a kiss, she felt even more sure about Flynn being an okay guy. Suddenly, as if sensing he was being looked at, he turned around and scanned the room. When he saw her, he smiled and waved. Tara shivered. He was coming toward them.

Yummy, Millicent sighed.

Millicent . . . don't mess with him.

I just said, yummy. I didn't say I was going to do anything.

Tara smiled at Flynn, but her mind was in a panic. The last thing she needed was for Millicent to make a scene.

Well! Really! I'm not a man-stealer, you know.

Could have fooled me, Tara thought, and then Flynn was at their booth.

"Hey, Moon girl."

"Hi," Tara said, then pointed at her uncle, who had managed to look both startled and territorial while his mouth was full of pie. "This is my Uncle Pat. Uncle Pat, this is Flynn O'Mara. We have two classes together."

Flynn stuck out his hand. "Pleased to meet you, sir."

The 'sir' struck a nice chord with Uncle Pat. "Um . . . yes, pleasure to meet any of Tara's friends," he said, and shook Flynn's hand.

"I see you're a lemon pie fan, too. It's the best here. My mom works, so I know what I'm talking about."

"Your Mom?"

Flynn pointed to Mona. "That's her. She's worked here since I started school full time."

"Mona is your mother, is she? Well now... that's something," Uncle Pat said, and then arched an eyebrow at Tara, who wisely played dumb. "Wow. What a small world," she said. "She was our waitress tonight."

Flynn seemed pleased.

Uncle Pat was clearly disconcerted. Tara sensed his dilemma. He felt like he should be disapproving of any young male hanging around her, but he was having a difficult time finding a way to criticize the son of a woman he liked.

Tara didn't quite know how to act. Uncle Pat was the most important man in her life—except maybe for Henry, who didn't quite qualify as a man anymore since he'd been dead for at least a century. But now there was Flynn. Yes, she was attracted to him, but she'd only known him a few days. There must surely be a timeline on these things.

"Would you like to have a seat?" Uncle Pat asked.

"It's really nice of you to ask, but I just came to pick up some food. I need to get back home and finish my homework. We've got a tough second period teacher, right, Tara?"

"Yes, tough," Tara echoed.

Millicent hissed, *Has your brain turned to mush?*

Tara managed a smile while wanting to wring Millicent's neck... if she only had one to wring. Bummer. How do you freak out on a wraith, anyway?

Freak? I am not a freak!

No, no, that's not what I meant, Tara thought, but it was too late.

The napkins on their table began flying out of the dispenser. In a panic, Tara grabbed the dispenser and clapped her hands over the napkins before Millicent could yank any more free.

"Wow. Talk about a draft in here," she said, and then clutched it against her chest while Pat and Flynn stared at her.

"I don't think there was a—"

"You know what, Uncle Pat? Flynn is right. That teacher is a bear about homework. I need to get home and finish mine, too, before it gets too late."

She smiled and laughed as if she'd said made the most amazing statement and waited for them to react. To her relief, they reacted exactly as she hoped and laughed with her, although there wasn't anything funny about what she'd said.

Pat had already paid the ticket Mona left at their table, but he began shelling out some more money for a tip, then nodded at Flynn as he stood up. "Nice to meet you, dude."

"You, too," Flynn said.

Tara got up, smiled at Flynn, and started to follow her uncle when Flynn called to her.

"Hey, Moon girl!"

She was still smiling as she turned. "Yes?"

He pointed at the napkin dispenser she had clutched against her chest.

"You might wanna leave that here."

She looked down, realized she was still holding the napkin dispenser, then rolled her eyes.

"Oh. Right. What was I thinking?"

She set it on the nearest table and then waved goodbye before heading to the door. She wouldn't look back for fear she'd see more napkins running amok. *Lunatic*, Prissy had called her. Maybe that twitch was closer to the truth than she knew. Tara's life was something of a lunatic existence.

She might have felt a little better if she'd known Flynn watched until the taillights of their car disappeared down the street, and that he thought about her smile as he walked home with his food.

The next morning, the Superintendent of Stillwater Public Schools issued a bulletin on local TV as well as radio, informing the high school students that yesterday's fire had been a localized electrical short and that the second flare-up had promptly been contained as well. The hope that school would be closed for another day soon faded as notice was given that classes would resume at their regular time. Tara wasn't the only one groaning at the news as students all over town began getting ready for school.

There was one other newsworthy item that caught Tara's attention. That of an attempted robbery at Beckman's Jewelry on Main Street, and the arrest of two men caught on the premises. She had a moment of satisfaction, knowing she was responsible for their arrest, but it didn't last. As she was eating breakfast, she felt the dark shadow's presence even before she saw it. Luckily, Uncle Pat was in the shower, getting ready for work.

She jumped up from the table with her fork in her hand, then grabbed the medal around her neck.

"Don't *even* think about it! I don't know what your deal is, but you have no business being ticked at me! You do *not* dis me like you did yesterday . . . ever again! Got that?"

The shadow swirled up toward the ceiling like a mini-tornado, then tried to move forward, but Tara's fury was stronger. She came at the shadow with her fork in one hand and her cross clutched in the other.

"If you wanted my help, all you had to do was communicate. Swiping through my head like a sneak thief won't cut it. Get out! Now!"

The shadow swirled, then disappeared so quickly it was startling.

"Good morning to you, too," Tara muttered, but her appetite was gone. She cleaned up her dishes, then went to her room to brush her teeth. It was almost time to leave.

A short while later she was on her way out the door with Flynn's denim jacket over her shoulder and her backpack slung over her arm.

"You sure you don't want a ride to school?" Pat asked.

"No. I like the walk," Tara said, as she pulled out her iPod. "It gives me time to listen to my tunes and I don't want to get there too early. Someone might think I liked it."

Pat laughed out loud, then waved as he drove away.

One to school. One to work. And one dark angry shadow left behind to contemplate more trouble.

The day passed without incident. After the throw-down she'd given the blonde mafia in Davis's car, no one seemed to want to mess with her. They were still stunned by what she'd said about their secrets, and wondering how she'd found out.

She gave Flynn his jacket in second hour, but not before half the class noticed the byplay. Before class was over, text messages had been sent to half the senior class stating Flynn O'Mara was after the lunatic girl, and that for all intents and purposes, she was letting him catch her.

All in all, it was a strange beginning to the first few weeks of Tara Luna's senior year.

Saturday finally arrived. No school.

It was the first thing Tara thought when she opened her eyes. This meant no classes to hurry off to. No gossip about her and Flynn to deal with. She rolled over, intent on trying for another hour or so of sleep, but Millicent had other ideas.

I know about the dark entity.

Tara sat straight up in bed. "You have my undivided attention."

If a ghost could smirk, Tara knew Millicent would be smirking. But Millicent didn't believe in wasting her energy and rarely appeared in anything more substantial than a wisp of pink smoke.

She's not evil.

"So, my dark entity is a she?"

She was murdered.

"Oh man," Tara whispered. "Now I get the anger, but why at me?"

You're living in her house.

"Well, great," Tara muttered. "But why hasn't she moved on?"

Because no one knows about the murder.

"Why?"

No one ever reported her missing, so they never found her body.

"And that's my fault, how?"

It's buried somewhere on this property.

"Front yard or back?"

I believe she stated the one to the west.

"That would be the back yard. Oh! Ugh! This is so not okay!"

Tara jumped out of bed, shuddering as the implications of what she'd just learned washed over her. "Why does this always happen to me?" *Um . . . excuse me, but I think her situation tops yours by a butt load.*

Tara sighed, then sank back down on the side of the bed. "You're right. I was just thinking out loud."

You still lose. You're alive and well, and she's not. She's worm food.

"Double ugh," Tara muttered, as she shivered again. "So, what does she expect me to do?"

Duh. Tell someone, dummy.

Tara ran her hands through her long, tangled hair, then got up and paced.

"Does she have a name?"

Actually, she's had several incarnations.

Tara frowned. "I'm talking about this last one, thank you."

A strange name. DeeDee Broyles.

"I deserve points for solving the mystery of my teacher's missing money and the robbery of a jewelry store. But now I have to get a shovel and start digging holes in the lawn to find a body? Have I missed anything here?"

Gratitude for a job well done?

Tara sighed. Right. She had asked Henry and Millicent to find out what the dark shadow was about.

"Thank you."

Humpf.

"Very much."

Much better.

"Do not freakin' push your luck. I'm the one with the degree of difficulty here."

Her dresser drawer came open and her panties began

flying across the room. She started to laugh. "While you're at it, get the dirty ones out of the clothes hamper and do the laundry. Don't forget to put the water on cold, please. Hot ruins the elastic."

With that, she headed for the shower. She had a lot to do before the day was over, including how to tell Uncle Pat that a lot more than squash had been planted in their back yard.

As soon as breakfast was over, Tara headed for the county courthouse to check some records, leaving Uncle Pat in the backyard with the lawn mower. *If he only knew what was buried under the grass,* she thought.

So she and Uncle Pat were living in what had been DeeDee Broyles' home. Tara needed to find out how long ago it was when the Broyles family owned the property, and if there were any members of the family still living in Stillwater. And why had no one ever reported DeeDee missing? A clerk at the courthouse helped her find the ledgers that were kept for registering property owners to particular addresses, then showed her how to look up the specifics. Tara thanked her for the help, then took out a pad and pen she'd brought with her and began making notes.

She and Uncle Pat were paying rent to a man named Sam Whiteside, so his name must be the most recent to be listed as owning their house. Then she began to trace ownership backward. From Whiteside to Fornier, and then there it was. Broyles. From 1946 to 1986, the house had belonged to the Broyles family. The last to own it was Emmit Broyles

Next she could hunt for a census record online, which should tell her all the names of family members in the Broyles household. It made no sense that DeeDee would disappear and no one would ever file a police report about it.

Tara gasped. Unless someone in her family was the murderer.

"I'm beginning to feel like a detective on CSI."

By the time she got out of the courthouse it was almost

noon. Her stomach was growling from hunger, but she didn't have time to eat. The sooner she got DeeDee's angry spirit pacified, the easier her life was going to be. She made a dash toward home. She needed to get online and find census records for the years that the Broyles family had owned the property, and see what came up there.

When she got home she heard the lawn mower running out back. Uncle Pat was still cleaning up. She grabbed a couple of cookies from the pantry, then headed for her room to get her laptop. She crawled into the middle of her bed, turned on the laptop, and began munching on one of her cookies as she waited for the system to come online. As soon as it did, she Googled *Census Records for the State of Oklahoma.*

After a few hits and misses, she finally found information relating to the years in which the Broyles family had owned her and Uncle Pat's house. Once again, she pulled out her little pad and pen to jot down the names. To her surprise, during the last census, there were only two recorded names for that family at that address. She assumed they were husband and wife.

"Emmit Lee Broyles. Sarah Delores Broyles." She frowned. "No DeeDee. Shoot. Maybe DeeDee was a visiting family member or . . . oh. Wait. DeeDee could be short for Delores."

At that point, her cell phone began to vibrate. She pulled it out of her pocket, saw there was a text message, and frowned again. Uncle Pat didn't know how to text her, so what was up with this? She opened the message.

Ewe R knot write.

Tara stifled a snort. Millicent thought she was all that because she could manipulate electricity to the point of being able to send text messages, but she so did not get the language.

"It's not ewe, that's a sheep. It's U, and . . . oh crap. Never mind. What am I not right about?"

Another text message appeared.

Not H and W. Sibs.

"Oh. Wow. Thanks," Tara muttered. "Emmit and DeeDee were brother and sister. Now to find out if Emmit

Broyles still lives in Stillwater, or if he is even still alive."

She rolled over to the side of the bed, grabbed the phone book from the table and flipped through the B's. Within minutes, she'd found an address for an Emmit Lee Broyles on Western Avenue.

"Could I be this lucky?" She made a note of the address.

Then she Googled Map Quest and downloaded a city map of Stillwater, looking for where this address was in connection to her address on Duck Street.

To her dismay, the address on Western was quite a distance to walk. She decided to make some lunch for her and Uncle Pat, then see if she could use the car this afternoon. Satisfied that she was on the trail of what was turning into quite a mystery, she headed for the kitchen.

Chapter Four

Tara was fired up and on a mission. It never occurred to her that she could be putting herself in mortal danger by asking the wrong questions of someone who might turn out to be a murder suspect. The only thing on her mind was solving a mystery and getting an angry entity out of their house.

The mailman was on the front porch as she hurried through the living room. She went outside just as he dropped the lid on the mail box.

"Hello, little lady," he said.

"Hi," Tara thanked him, fished the mail from the box, and headed for the back yard.

She wondered what it was going to look like once it was cleared out. It was creepy to know there was a body buried here. But it wasn't like there'd be a tombstone or anything. Murderers weren't in the habit of calling attention to their deeds, and according to her information it had been years and years since the Broyles family had lived here.

She stepped outside on the back porch, then smiled with surprise. It looked really great. Uncle Pat hadn't just mowed the grass. He'd clipped bushes, trimmed tree limbs—even trained some wild ivy vines so that they were now climbing through the slats of a small white arbor in one corner of the yard. Mowing had uncovered something all right, but not a grave. It had revealed a narrow, winding path paved with natural stones. She could only imagine what it must have once looked like, with flowers blooming in the beds and birds and butterflies flitting about.

Uncle Pat saw her and waved, then cut the engine on the mower and started toward the house.

"The yard looks amazing, Uncle Pat."

Her praise brought a smile to his face as he pulled a handkerchief from his back pocket and wiped the sweat off his brow.

"Quite a little surprise, wasn't it?" he said, as he stepped up on the porch, then he pointed to the north corner of the yard. "See that little arbor back there?"

"Uh-huh."

"There's an old iron bench in the shed out back. I'll drag it out and scrub it up a bit and then put it out there under the arbor. It'll make a nice place to sit in the evenings."

"That'll be great, Uncle Pat. I like this house, and the school has possibilities, although I don't have to put up with it for more than a year. After that, I'm off to college. Do you think we might actually stay here? Oklahoma State University is right here in Stillwater. It has a great rep and it would save a lot of money if I could still live at home and attend classes."

His expression fell. Tara sensed his sorrow. She'd been his "little girl" for so long, it was difficult for him to imagine what life would be like without her. And he knew she didn't like his gypsy ways. She hoped he'd stay put for a few years, motivated by the idea that she'd live at home while going to college, if he remained in Stillwater.

"Maybe so. Maybe so. Being a city employee means a good retirement plan, and I don't mind reading meters. In fact, I sort of like the job. So we'll see how it goes, okay?" he said, and then put an arm around her shoulders as they walked inside. "I'm hungry, how about you?"

That was more of a promise than she'd gotten out of him in years, and for the moment, she had to be satisfied with his answer.

"Starved. I'll make sandwiches. Want some soup heated up, too?"

"Yes, please. There are some cans of chicken noodle and vegetable beef. You choose. I'm gonna go wash up."

Tara washed her hands in the sink and then got the lunch meat and mustard from the fridge and the bread from the cabinet. She was layering slices of pastrami on the bread when the back door suddenly came open. The hair rose on the back of her neck, and she knew before she turned around that the dark shadow was back.

She dropped the mustard-smeared knife onto the counter as she turned.

"Just in time for lunch, DeeDee. Do you want mustard or mayo?"

Tara's heart was thumping erratically. She didn't know what had made her say that, but now that she knew the circumstances of the dark shadow's passing and understood the anger that drove it, she wasn't afraid of it anymore.

The shadow shifted in the opening, then slid toward the pantry. Tara held her breath. Either the dishes would start flying at her, or it was the beginning of a new friendship. Whatever happened, it was DeeDee's call.

Tara waited for a second, and when nothing happened, she shrugged and turned back around, reached for the can opener, then took two cans of soup from the cabinet.

"The back yard looks great, doesn't it? I'll bet it was beautiful when you lived here as a child. Did your Mother have a vegetable garden, too? There's certainly room for one."

Nothing hit her in the back of the head, and she didn't hear anything either. That gave her the courage to continue.

"I'm heating the vegetable beef soup. It will go good with pastrami, I think. It's one of Uncle Pat's favorites."

There was a thump behind her. She took a slow breath, looked over her shoulder, then gasped. The dark shadow was gone, and in its place was the wispy image of a young woman with sad eyes and short, curly hair. She was wearing a simple dress and flat-heeled shoes. She pointed at Tara, then put her hand over her heart.

Tara sighed. "I'm sorry, too," she said. "I know this was once your house. I know you were murdered. I'm trying to help. Can you tell me who killed you? Why weren't you reported as missing? Where did they bury your body?"

"Who are you talking to?" Uncle Pat said, as he strode back into the kitchen.

Tara stifled a groan. DeeDee disappeared.

"Oh, myself, I guess," Tara said, and then dumped the soup into the pan and set it on the stove. "Do we have any dill pickles? I made pastrami sandwiches."

"Yep. Got some the other day. I'll get the pickles. You stir the soup."

Tara finished heating the soup and dished it up while her uncle carried the sandwiches to the table, then filled their glasses with lemonade. They sat down together and began to eat. "Uncle Pat, may I use the car this afternoon? I need to do some research and it's too far to walk."

"Yes, sure honey," he said, as he dug a pickle out of the pickle jar. "Want one?"

"No, thanks, I'm good," Tara finished off the last bite of her sandwich.

"By the way," Pat said. "Have you seen my glasses? I thought I laid them here on the table before I went outside, but I can't find them anywhere."

"I'll look in a sec," Tara said, as she carried her dirty dishes to the sink. "Maybe they're in the living room," she said. "I'll look there."

"I already did," Pat said. "But you might as well have a go at it, too."

Tara stomped into the living room, then shoved her finger into the air in a gesture of defiance and hissed in a low, angry voice.

"Henry! Glasses! In my hand now!"

She held out her hand and closed her eyes. Seconds later, she felt them land in the middle of her palm and quickly curled her fingers around them as she looked up.

"I am not going to thank you for something you shouldn't have taken in the first place," she whispered. "Please don't do it again."

A magazine slid off the coffee table onto the floor.

"And pick that up!" she growled, as she stomped out of the room and back into the kitchen, holding the glasses in a gesture of triumph. "Look what I found," she said.

"For goodness sake. Where were they?"

"On the coffee table ... under an open magazine," she said, irked that she'd had to lie. If Uncle Pat wasn't so closed-minded about her being psychic, it would be a lot easier.

She was anxious to see Emmit Broyles face to face—to see if she would pick up anything from his behavior or thoughts. She might be all wrong about what she'd been thinking, but it was definitely strange that someone's sister would go missing and no one seemed to care.

"Okay. I'm off to do research," she said, gave her Uncle Pat a kiss and a hug, took the car keys from the counter, and headed for the driveway.

"Drive carefully," he called.

"I will," Tara answered, then smiled. He always said that and she always answered the same way which cracked her up. Like, if anyone was planning to drive like a maniac, they would admit to it before they left? What kind of logic was that?

Thanks to MapQuest, she knew where Western Avenue was, and headed South down Duck street to 12th Avenue, then 12th Avenue to Western, while her head was spinning with opening scenarios as to how she would greet Emmit Broyles.

Her confusion was compounded by the sudden appearance of Henry, who popped up on the hood of her car like a hood ornament. If he knew how distracting it was to try and drive through traffic with a ghost staring at you through the windshield, he would have at least gotten into the car beside her.

"Henry! Move! I can't be looking at you when I'm supposed to be paying attention to traffic!"

Henry popped out of sight and then into the seat beside her so fast that she jumped.

"Crap! You scared me." She braked for a red light.

Don't go, Millicent said.

Tara rolled her eyes. Now Millicent was in the back seat, adding her two cents into the situation.

"Look you two. I am not sharing the rest of my life with an angry entity. DeeDee deserves some justice. All I'm going to do is talk to her brother. Either I'll get some info from him, or I won't."

You can get murdered like DeeDee.

Tara's heart skipped a beat. "Are you saying he killed her?"

We don't know.

Tara frowned. "Why don't you know?"

Because DeeDee doesn't know who killed her, either.

"Oh great. Why couldn't this be easy?" Then another thing occurred to her. "Does she know exactly where she's buried?"

She used to.

Tara snorted lightly. "Either she does or she doesn't."

The yard doesn't look like it used to.

"You mean . . . like, maybe she was buried under the rose bushes, or something like that, only the rose bushes aren't there any more? Is that what you mean?"

Ta da!

"A simple yes would have been sufficient," Tara muttered, and then her heart gave an erratic thump as she saw the house number she'd been looking for. "We're here!" she announced, and turned up into the driveway and parked.

The house was a plain red brick with green shutters. The grass was neatly mowed and the small flower beds up around the porch were full of blooming pansies and periwinkles. There was a hummingbird feeder on the south end of the porch and two huge pots of Boston ferns on either side of the bottom step. It didn't look like the house of a killer. Then she frowned. Exactly what was a killer's house supposed to look like?

This isn't a good idea.

"Yes, Millicent, I know. We've already had this discussion." Tara got out of the car and headed for the front door.

Henry kept darting in front of her, then moving just before she'd walk through him, then back in her path again.

"Yes. Yes. I get the message. But you've also gotten mine. Now both of you back off and let me do my thing!"

The moment they disappeared, worry settled firmly at the

back of her mind. No one knew where she was. If she opened Pandora's box with her questions, she didn't want to find herself planted in this back yard like DeeDee had been planted in hers. But it was the thought of poor DeeDee, unsettled and in unhallowed ground, that made her keep walking—right up the steps, and then ringing the bell.

She listened as the chimes echoed within the interior of the house, then patiently waited for someone to answer. And she waited. And waited, then rang again.

After all the fuss and bother coming over here, this was something of a letdown. She peeked into the windows, then exhaled in frustration and headed back to the car. She was all the way off the porch when she heard the door suddenly open behind her.

"Can I help you?"

The voice was obviously from someone of the elder generation—a little shaky and weak. She turned abruptly.

The woman in the doorway looked like a good puff of wind would blow her away. She was stooped from the weight of her years, and verging on skinny, although her navy blue dress gave the impression of substance. Her gray hair was obviously long, because she wore it braided, then wound up on the top of her head. Fragile, wire-rimmed glasses perched on the bridge of her slightly hooked nose, and the hand that was clutching the cane on which she was leaning had some serious bling on every finger.

"Does Emmit Broyles live here?" Tara asked.

"Why, yes, he does. I'm his wife, Flora."

"Is he here, Mrs. Broyles? I'd like to speak to him."

The old woman frowned. "He's out back in the garden, but he doesn't like to be disturbed."

Tara hurried back up the steps. "I really need to talk to him," she said.

"About what?"

"His sister, DeeDee."

The old woman frowned. "Oh, you must be mistaken. He doesn't have a sister named DeeDee. In fact, Emmit doesn't have any siblings at all."

Tara frowned. According to the census info she'd found, she knew different. "Would you just ask him if he'd speak with me? Tell him that my uncle and I are living in his family's old house."

"The one on Duck Street?" Flora asked.

"Yes, ma'am."

Flora frowned. "Wait here," she said, and then shut the door in Tara's face.

Tara could hear her scooting across the floor and knew it would take a few minutes before she'd even make it to the back of the house to deliver the message. She shoved her hands in her pockets and then started to sit down on the steps when Millicent's voice cautioned otherwise.

I wouldn't turn my back if I were you.

Tara flinched, then turned and faced the doorway. "If you don't know anything about this guy, then why do you insist on making such a fuss?" she muttered.

Oddly enough, she didn't answer, which bothered Tara more than if she'd continued her complaints. Then suddenly Tara began to hear footsteps approaching and unconsciously, her fingers curled into fists.

The door opened.

Whatever Tara had been expecting, it wasn't this.

Emmit Broyles was the physical opposite of his wife, Flora. Where she was frail and stooped, he was tall with a military posture. His shoulders were so wide that he barely fit in the doorway, and the extra weight he carried just made his presence even more impressive. But it wasn't his size that Tara picked up on. It was the angry glare in his eyes and the jut of his jaw. She felt the antagonism before he ever opened his mouth, but oddly enough, she couldn't get anything from his thoughts. Those were completely shut down.

Hmm, a man with secrets, she thought, and then smiled politely.

"Mr. Broyles . . . Emmit Broyles?"

"What do you want?"

Nothing like getting right to the point. Tara took a step forward, just to show him she wasn't intimidated by his behavior.

"My uncle and I are renting the house that used to belong to your family . . . the house on Duck Street."

"So?"

She shuffled her feet, pretending to be a little embarrassed, she looked up at him from the corner of her eyes and played stupid.

"So . . . when you lived there, did either you or your sister, DeeDee, ever feel like the house was haunted?"

If she'd slapped him in the face with a dead fish, he couldn't have looked any more shocked.

"What did you say?"

"Haunted. As in ghosts. I didn't think I believed in such stuff until we moved there. But I'd swear there's a ghost in the house and she's not happy we're there. I've been trying to find out some history to the place . . . maybe so I could help the ghost move on . . . you know, like on *The Ghost Whisperer.* I just love that show. Do you ever watch it? Jennifer Love Hewitt is like, so gorgeous and she's always helping spirits pass over. So, I was thinking maybe I could do the same thing and wanted to talk to your sister, DeeDee, because women are usually more open to talking about things like this, but no one seems to know where she's gone."

His voice was barely above a whisper. "I don't have a sister."

"Oh! I'm so sorry! I didn't realize she'd passed away."

"No . . . no. I don't have a sister."

Tara frowned. "But that's not what the court records state. That's how I found you, you know. Records. At the courthouse."

Emmit took a step outside, pulling the door shut behind him, then moved until there was less than a foot between them.

"I don't know what you're game is, but you need to get off my property and don't come back."

He loomed over her, using his size to intimidate. It was

working. Then suddenly, Tara felt Millicent's presence and knew she'd better move before Millicent went into action.

"I don't have a game and there's no need to bully me. It's upsetting enough living in a house with a ghost. I thought with you and your family living there for so long, you would be able to help me. I'm sorry I bothered you."

She lifted her chin and turned abruptly, pretending indignation as she headed for her car.

Suddenly, she heard Emmit Broyles shout.

Tara turned around just as the old man began flailing his arms wildly, ducking and hopping and trying to get to the front door.

"What the hell?" he roared, as the porch was suddenly filled with wasps, diving at him from every direction. As if that wasn't enough, the blossoms on the flowers in the flower bed suddenly spewed into the air like lava erupting out of a volcano.

Tara grinned. *Way to go*, Millicent.

Get yourself in the car and go home.

For once, Millicent's advice was on target. Tara jumped in, locked the doors, and then drove away.

"I think that went well," she said, as she reached down to turn on the radio, but before she could, it came on by itself.

She didn't recognize the song, but some rapper kept repeating the words, *run, boy run*. She hoped it wasn't the universe trying to tell her something. What she needed to do was get back home and try to communicate with DeeDee again. She wasn't sure how to go about finding her grave, but she had to figure something out. It was the only thing she could think of that would convince the police that there had been a crime committed—that DeeDee Broyles had been murdered—most likely by her own brother.

Unfortunately, the weekend didn't go as Tara wanted. After that brief moment in the kitchen when DeeDee had revealed her true self, she'd suddenly made herself scarce. Even Henry and Millicent stayed absent. Tara was beginning to feel abandoned.

On Sunday she slept in, then Uncle Pat insisted on taking her back to Eskimo Joe's for lunch. Tara now knew for certain he had a thing for Mona O'Mara. To her relief, Mona wasn't working the noon shift, which meant Tara could enjoy her food without thinking about Uncle Pat hooking up with Flynn's mother. That was enough to make a girl freak.

Sunday afternoon, Tara headed to the backyard, but no matter how many times she walked it, she couldn't see anything that would lead her to where DeeDee's body was buried. And, she kept sending DeeDee messages to check in, but DeeDee remained AWOL. As frustrating as it was to wait, she didn't have any other options.

When the alarm went off Monday morning, Tara bounced out of bed, expecting Henry to be sitting on the foot of her bed. Within seconds, she knew she was still alone.

"Fine," she muttered, and headed to the shower.

By the time she got to school, the chip on her shoulder was riding high and wide. How positively bunk was it to be such an outcast that even *dead* people refused to hang with her? Just because she'd told them to back off didn't mean she'd meant *forever*.

She was on her way to her locker when the blonde mafia turned a corner and came down the hall toward her. They were walking three across, expecting everyone else to make way for them, which they did. But Tara wasn't in the mood to bow and scrape. She didn't miss a step or break stride. She just set her jaw and kept walking.

Right up to the three blonde cheerleaders. Until they were standing face to face.

"Hey! Lunatic! Can't you see we're walking here?"

"Move," Tara said.

"Ooh, I am so scared," Prissy said, and rolled her eyes.

Tara leaned forward until her mouth was only inches away from her ear.

"You cheated on your test Friday and your teacher knows

it."

Prissy's face turned white as her eyes widened. This was the second time Tara had revealed something no one but Prissy could possibly know. "What are you . . . a witch?" Prissy whispered.

"I said . . . move."

"What did she say to you, Prissy? Did she threaten you?" Bethany asked. "I'll get the principal. She'll—"

"No," Prissy said quickly as she moved aside. "Let it go."

Tara walked between them and kept on going without looking back. The stand-down hadn't gone unnoticed, and by the time Tara got to first hour, word was spreading. Tara Luna *was* a witch, as in some kind of Satan-worshiping goat-sacrificer, although real wiccans weren't into that stuff. Mrs. Farmer kept giving her curious looks. Even though everything Tara had told her about her babysitter had turned out to be true, she'd hadn't mentioned any of the end results to Tara. Tara sighed. Mrs. Farmer probably believed she was a witch, too. It wasn't the first time this had happened to Tara, and it wouldn't be the last. The worst thing about it was seeing the look of shock on Flynn O'Mara's face when he walked in the classroom for their second period class. As if that wasn't enough, instead of talking to her like he usually did, he ducked his head and looked away. She smelled the scent of his aftershave and wanted to cry as he slid into the seat behind her.

Fine, Tara thought. *Join the club. Nobody else wants to be friends with me, either.*

Cold, Tara. We're still here.

Millicent. Tara had never been so glad to hear that nagging little voice in her life.

"The word isn't *cold.* It's *chill.* You say, 'Chill,' when you want someone to calm down."

Whatever.

"Are you talking to yourself, Lunatic?"

Tara looked up. It was secretly bulemic Mel, the third and least vocal member of the blonde mafia.

"I'd tell you to drop dead, but hey . . . if I'm a witch, then that might be called a murder attempt, wouldn't it?"

Mel's smirk fell like a curtain. "Stay away from me," she mumbled, and scurried to her desk.

Tara slumped in her desk.

Why do you do that?

Do what? Tara thought.

Antagonize them. They're idiots, you know.

Yes, I know.

They're going to keep spreading rumors about you.

I can't control other people's behavior.

The last bell rang, the teacher closed the classroom door, and the class began. About thirty minutes into the class, Tara began getting a panicky feeling. Something was wrong somewhere close, but she couldn't pick up on what was happening.

The teacher got up from the desk and began writing an assignment on the board. Tara began copying down the instructions, when all of a sudden she wasn't looking at the words on her paper any more. She was seeing a scene unfolding inside a bathroom. There was a kid on the floor and he was having a seizure. There were more than a half dozen bathrooms in the building. She had no idea which one, but she knew as well as she knew her own name that the boy was dying.

She bolted out of the seat and headed for the teacher as fast as she could go.

"Mrs. Wyatt, I need to be excused."

The teacher turned, then frowned. "Can't you wait," she whispered.

"No, ma'am. It's an emergency. Please. I've got to go."

"All right then, but—"

Tara was out the door before she finished the sentence and running up the hall toward the teacher's lounge. She needed help fast, and knew that was where the teachers spent their prep hour. She burst into the door without knocking. Coach Jones and several other teachers looked up from their papers, some were frowning. Others just appeared surprised.

"Please. You've got to help me!" she cried. "A boy is having a seizure in one of the boy's bathrooms. He's going to die if he doesn't get help."

They were on their feet in seconds.

"Where is he?" Coach shouted.

"I don't know. I just know he's on the floor in a boy's bathroom. Please. You have to hurry."

"Wait! What do you mean you don't know? If you don't know where he is, then how do you know what's happening?"

"I just do," she cried, and then ran out of the room with the teachers right behind her.

"I'll take the south end," Coach said.

'I'll go with you," a teacher offered.

The Spanish teacher and the debate coach jumped up. "We'll take the north wing."

Tara's heart was pounding so fast she could hardly breathe. *Oh God, please don't let him die,* Tara thought.

He's on the north end.

Millicent! Why didn't you tell me earlier?

"He's at the north end!" she screamed, and started running.

Two of the teachers did a quick about face and followed Tara, who was running down the hall as fast as she could. She could feel the boy's heartbeat ebbing. The fear that they'd be too late was overwhelming.

Then she saw Coach Jones come flying out of a boys' bathroom with a look of panic on his face.

"In here!" he yelled. "And call 911," then pivoted and ran back inside.

Tara flew in behind him and slid down on her knees beside the boy.

"Is he still breathing?" she asked.

The coach was checking for a pulse.

"No . . . God help us, no. He's not."

"I know CPR," Tara offered, but before she could help, another pair of teachers came into the bathroom on the run and pushed her out of the way.

They began performing CPR while another was on the phone. Tara flattened herself against the wall, trying to stay out of the way when she sensed someone standing beside her. She glanced over and found herself staring at the spirit of the boy who was lying on the floor.

Is that me?

Tara nodded.

Am I dead?

"I think . . . I think you're somewhere in-between," Tara whispered.

There was a sad expression on the boy's face. *I don't want to die.*

"Then go back," Tara said.

The spirit disappeared. Tara didn't know whether he'd passed into the light, or if he'd gone back into his body, but from where she was standing, she didn't see any signs of life. Her legs were shaking and there were tears in her eyes. She'd never seen anyone die before, and even though she saw ghosts on a daily basis, watching someone become one was startling.

Then all of a sudden, the boy on the floor gasped, then coughed and groaned.

"He's breathing on his own!" the coach cried.

"I've got a pulse," the other teacher said. "It's not good, but it's there."

"I hear the ambulance," Tara said.

The coach looked up at her, as if just remembering she was still there. "Go down and show them where we're at."

"Yes, sir," Tara said, and gladly ran out of the bathroom, down the hall, and then out the front door.

After the EMTs entered the bathroom, loaded the boy up on a stretcher, then headed back to the ambulance, Tara felt better. At least, whatever happened was out of her hands. She started back to her classroom, and then halfway down the hall her legs went out from under her. She sank down against the wall to keep from falling, then slid to the floor and started to sob.

She was still crying when someone touched her on the

shoulder. She looked up. It was Coach Jones.

"Are you all right?"

"Yes, sir," she said, swiping at the tears still on her face.

He squatted down beside her, then took a handkerchief out of his pocket and handed it to her.

"You did good," he said.

Tara nodded, wiped her eyes, then blew her nose.

"What's your name?" Coach Jones asked.

"Tara Luna."

"So, Tara Luna, tell me something. How did you know?"

She blew her nose again, and then handed him his handkerchief.

He grinned, then shook his head. "You keep it."

"Oh. Yeah. Sorry," she said, thinking about how many times she'd blown her nose in it, and stood up.

"Hey! Tara!"

She stopped, then turned back around. "Yeah, Coach?"

"You didn't answer my question."

Tara sighed. "You're not gonna like the answer."

"Try me," he said softly.

"Sometimes I just . . . I just know stuff, okay?"

He followed her for a few steps without comment, but as she started back to her room, he touched her shoulder.

"About this knowing stuff?"

"Yeah, what about it?" she asked.

"Are we talking psychic, here?"

"You might be, but I'm not going to talk about it," Tara said.

"I see," Coach Jones said.

"Sometimes I wish I didn't," Tara said quietly, and then walked away.

Chapter Five

Tara was quiet when she walked back into the classroom. She wouldn't look at anybody. She just slid into her seat and picked her book back up.

"Hey, Lunatic . . . what was going on?" someone asked.

Tara shrugged. They'd obviously heard the ambulance. But she wasn't going to volunteer anything. She just wanted this day over with as fast as possible.

A few minutes later, the bell rang. She was putting her book and folders into her book bag when she heard Flynn's voice behind her.

"Hey, Tara . . . how's it going?"

She looked up.

It was the tears in her eyes that hit Flynn like a fist to the stomach.

"What happened?" he asked.

"Which time?" she drawled. "When everyone started calling me a witch, or when I ran out of the room?"

Then she walked away without giving him time to answer. By shunning her earlier, his star had already dimmed. Whether it was beyond redemption or not remained to be seen, but right now she was too rattled to deal with it.

She moved through the rest of her morning classes with her head down and her eyes on her feet. She didn't look up. Didn't want to see the whispering. Didn't want to know what was happening.

It's time for lunch and you're going the wrong way.

"I'm not hungry, okay?" Tara muttered, as she shoved her back pack in her locker and headed for the front doors.

The fresh air felt good on her face. She paused at the head of the steps, glanced around the campus, then headed for a tree at the far corner of the school yard. There was a small patch of shade and enough distance between her and the building that hopefully, no one would notice her until it was time to go in.

From a distance she would be anonymous, just another teenager, tall and leggy, wearing a loose-fitting tee and a pair of faded jeans. The breeze lifted the lengths of her long dark hair off the back of her neck as she walked, cooling her skin and her senses. By the time she got to the shade tree, she was feeling better. She sat down on the bench beneath the tree, then pulled her knees up under her chin, rested her forehead on her knees and then closed her eyes.

You saved his life. Millicent's voice was gentle.

Tara didn't answer. She felt the air shift slightly and knew Henry had joined her, too.

Their presence was soothing. She could feel the love and concern, which made her more teary than ever. She had to get hold of herself. The last thing she wanted was for the blonde mafia to see her all weak and weepy. What a pitiful heap she was. Two ghosts were her only BFFs and she'd been branded a witch. School sucked and she wanted this year to be over.

Then her cell phone began to vibrate in her pocket.

She pulled it out and answered absently.

"Hello, Uncle Pat."

"We heard an ambulance had been dispatched to high school. I was just checking on you."

A sob caught in the back of her throat as she reminded herself she still had Uncle Pat, too.

"I'm fine," she said.

"You don't sound fine," he said. "You sound like you've been crying."

"Oh. Well. I am sort of teary," she said. "I mean, it was scary to see that boy being carried out on a stretcher."

"What happened to him?"

"I heard that he had a seizure. He didn't have a pulse when they found him, but I heard they did CPR successfully. I hope he's going to be okay."

"Okay, honey," he said. "Sorry to bother. Just have to

make sure my best girl is okay, you know."

"Yes, Uncle Pat, I know, and I appreciate it, more than you know."

"Yes, well," he said, and cleared his throat. "I'd better get back to work. See you this evening."

"Yeah. This evening," Tara said, and then dropped her phone back into her pocket.

She leaned back against the tree and then looked up. Henry was sitting on a tree limb, looking down. She grinned.

"You look like a squirrel."

He frowned, then vaporized.

Tara sighed. "Sorry. I didn't mean to insult you," she said.

An acorn dropped on her head. She laughed. "Okay, I had that coming."

"There she is!"

Tara heard the shout and turned around, then groaned. "Why me?"

Bethany, Prissy, and Mel were heading her way.

I've got this one, Millicent chortled.

Tara sighed. Ever the faithful Millicent. It felt good that someone—even if it was only a small wraith with a pinkish tinge—had her back. She folded her arms across her chest and leaned back to watch.

Prissy was beyond angry. Yes, she'd been caught cheating; now she was off the cheerleading team, and totally blamed Tara for it. Despite the fact that Tara wasn't even in the class where she'd cheated on her test, Prissy had decided that Tara was the snitch who told on her.

"You ought to just let it be," Mel said, unwilling to get any closer to Tara Luna. "That girl might cast another spell on us."

Bethany was reluctant to get involved. She liked being the center of the cheerleader universe, but she didn't like being associated with losers, and right now, Prissy was a loser. It wasn't so much that she'd cheated on her test as it was she'd gotten caught at it. Bad, bad, karma.

"Davis is waiting for me," Bethany said. "I'll see you guys at cheerleading practice this evening." Then she realized what she'd just said and looked at Prissy. "Sorry. I didn't mean . . . " Bethany sighed. She didn't need to apologize for Prissy's screw-ups. "Later, Mel."

"Yeah, later," Mel said, but hung back as Prissy started across the campus toward the bench where Tara was sitting.

Prissy stopped, then looked back. "Well, aren't you coming?" she asked.

Mel shook her head. "You need to leave Tara alone. I'm scared of her."

Prissy was furious. Her carefully plotted world was slipping out from under her, and it was all because of the lunatic. Everything had been fine until she came.

She headed for Tara with her head up, her arms swinging at her side in an opposite motion with her short jerky stride— like a drum major marching without a band.

Just a little bit closer.

"Don't hurt her," Tara warned.

I won't draw blood.

"That's all I ask," Tara muttered.

Prissy was within twenty feet of where Tara was sitting when she started mouthing off, calling Tara a snitch, and a witch and a liar. Prissy was gearing up for more when she was suddenly engulfed in a swirl of grass, dirt and leaves.

She shrieked, and then covered her eyes as the air continued to boil around her.

A bunch of students who were hanging around the front doors heard her scream. They turned to look, and then began to laugh and point, thinking she'd just gotten caught in a dust devil. Those were common in Oklahoma and not unlike minitornadoes, only dust devils always dissipated as quickly as they formed, and the only thing they blew away were bits of grass and dirt.

Tara stood up, watching as the dust devil engulfed Prissy. Millicent was outdoing herself, which meant she was really angry on Tara's behalf.

Prissy turned around to run, assuming she would run out of the dust devil within a step or two. But it didn't happen. Every step Prissy took, the dust devil moved with her. It didn't take long for the students to realize this was not normal. In fact, it was so out of the ordinary, it was downright spooky.

Prissy was running and screaming and waving her arms above her head.

"Help! Help! Make her stop! Make the witch stop!"

When everyone began hearing what Prissy was saying, they looked to where Tara had been standing, but she was gone. At that point, even the doubtful began to believe. Maybe Tara Luna *was* a witch. What else could explain what was happening?

Tara hurried through a side door, took her backpack from her locker, and headed for third period, even though it was early. All she had to do was get through the day and pray for no more excitement. She should have known it wouldn't be that easy.

"Miss Luna."

Tara turned to see the principal, Mrs. Crabtree, standing the doorway of her office.

"Yes, ma'am?"

"I would like to talk to you."

"Yes, ma'am," Tara said, and sighed. Of course Mrs. Crabtree wanted to talk to her. Everyone wanted a piece of her. She was the freakin' witch of Stillwater High.

She followed the principal into her office.

"Please, have a seat," Mrs. Crabtree said, and pointed to a chair on the other side of her desk.

Tara sat, put her backpack on the floor next to her feet and waited.

Mrs. Crabtree sat down, rested her elbows on the table and, for a few quiet moments, just looked at Tara.

Tara wasn't going to fall for that. She'd faced ghosts and dark shadows on a daily basis. A principal whose only strong point was staring to elicit a guilty conscience was a piece of cake.

"Talk to me," Mrs. Crabtree finally said.

Tara frowned. "About what?"

"How did you know Corey Palmer was having a seizure?"

Ahh, that one. Okay. She could play along. "I didn't know his name," she said, then added. "It's hard to explain."

"I've been an educator for twenty-three years. I've heard every explanation you can imagine in every context you can imagine. Try me."

"Sometimes I just know stuff."

"How do you know stuff?"

"I'm psychic?"

To Mrs. Crabtree's credit, she only blinked twice before her mouth sort of dropped. And even though she did it without thinking, the fact that she suddenly took her elbows off the table and leaned *away* from Tara, spoke volumes.

"Really?" Mrs. Crabtree said.

"Yes, ma'am, but I'd appreciate it if you sort of kept this under wraps. It makes my life difficult enough as it is."

Mrs. Crabtree frowned. "You're serious? I mean . . . you're actually asking me to believe this?"

"No, ma'am. I'm not asking you to believe it. I just answered your question."

"And what if I don't believe you?"

Tara swallowed past the knot in her throat and prayed she didn't wimp out and cry again. Showing weakness to the enemy wasn't wise.

"It's your call," Tara said. "By the way, is the kid . . . you said his name was Corey? Is he okay?"

"Yes, he is, actually."

"That's great," Tara said, nodded.

The principal frowned.

Millicent whispered, *I want a piece of her, too.*

"Lord, no," Tara muttered. "I'm in enough trouble, already."

"I'm sorry. What did you say?" the principal asked.

Tara rolled her eyes. "I . . . uh, I wasn't talking to you."

Mrs. Crabtree's eyebrows rose. "You talk to yourself?"

"No, ma'am. I was talking to Millicent. And before you

ask, she's a ghost. I've known her forever."

"My dear. I had no idea," Mrs. Crabtree muttered. "I want you to bring your parents in tomorrow. We need to get you into therapy so—"

The cold cup of coffee on the principal's desk suddenly levitated in the air, then turned upside down in her lap.

"Millicent! I told you not to," Tara wailed.

Mrs. Crabtree's mouth was open, but nothing was coming out.

"I'm so sorry," Tara said, as she jumped up and grabbed a handful of paper towels from the adjoining bathroom. "It was because you doubted me. Millicent is very protective."

She handed the principal the wad of paper towels and then started to sit down when two pens and a pencil on the principal's desk suddenly shot straight up in the air. Then they flew across the room like mini-missiles before sticking in a cork bulletin board like darts.

"Dear Lord, have mercy!" Mrs. Crabtree shrieked, staring at Tara in disbelief.

Tara sighed. "Back off, Millicent."

I think that went well.

"I'll just bet you do," Tara muttered. She picked up her backpack and started out the door. Then something about Mrs. Crabtree nudged at Tara's instincts. She paused then looked back. "Um . . . Mrs. Crabtree, you live in the house where you grew up, don't you?"

The principal's hands were over her mouth to keep from screaming, and the expression in her eyes was just shy of hysterics. But she managed to nod.

"You should probably know that your mother hid a whole bunch of money under the floor board in her bedroom. She also hid more in a shoe box in the attic. She put it where you keep Christmas ornaments. It's in an old trunk underneath a couple of quilts. You should retrieve it all soon. A mouse has been nibbling on the money under the floor for about a month."

"My mother has been dead for twenty-three years. Longer

than you've been alive. How do you know this?"

"I'm psychic, remember. Are we done?"

"Yes."

The bell rang.

"I'd better get to third period."

"Yes."

"So, you won't be mentioning anything we've said to anyone, will you?"

"Probably not.

"Thank you, Mrs. Crabtree. My life is complicated enough without everyone grilling me about their future or what numbers to pick for the lottery, and stuff like that."

Then she turned around and left the office before anything else went flying.

Tara waited until most of the other students were gone before leaving her last class of the day, then dragged her feet all the way to her locker. This day had totally sucked. She kept telling herself that none of it really mattered because a boy who would have died, was alive. And, the principal could have suspended her for claiming to be psychic then performing magic tricks—flying pens and spilling coffee—but she hadn't. Still, Tara felt defeated—drained of all the joy she'd started the day with. She didn't know why her path in this life was supposed to be so hard. Growing up without parents. Being born both psychic and a medium, as if having one bizarre "gift" wasn't hard enough. So many problems. So little time to solve them.

She tossed her folder into the locker, shuffled books out of her backpack, and put some others in that she would have to study from tonight, then slammed the locker shut. The sound echoed down the hall. A janitor looked up briefly.

Tara waved. "Sorry," she said.

He nodded, then went back to sweeping.

Tara slung her backpack over her shoulder and started toward the front door. As she exited the building, a girl came up the steps to meet her.

"Hey . . . aren't you Tara Luna?"

Tara froze. Now what? She eyed the girl curiously, checking out her attitude. She didn't pick up on any antagonism, which was a first.

"Yes. Who wants to know?" Tara asked, then winced. That sounded too defensive. But it was too late to take back.

"My name is Nikki Scott. Corey Palmer is my boyfriend. I just got back from the hospital. He told me what you did today and I just wanted to say thank you for saving his life."

The kindness was so unexpected, she was caught off guard. She tried to speak, and then found herself swallowing around a lump in her throat, instead.

"Yes, well . . . I'm glad I could help."

Nikkie pointed toward the parking lot. Most of the cars were gone in the student parking lot, except for a truck and a gray Chevy Trailblazer. "The SUV is mine. Do you need a ride home?"

For pity's sake, say yes!

Millicent was still trying to run her life. Only this time, she had a good point.

"You sure you want to be seen with a witch?" Tara asked.

Nikki shrugged. "That is so lame. Not every one at Stillwater High is in Bethany's stupid gossip clan."

"She hasn't been so bad," Tara said. "But Prissy is another story."

"Prissy wants to be Bethany. Bethany feeds off the power trip that being head cheerleader gives her.

"Now, do you want that ride home or not?"

"Yes, that would be great," Tara said. "I live over on Duck Street."

"No problem," Nikki said, and together, they walked toward the parking lot.

By the time Nikki let her out at the driveway, Tara had learned that Nikki had two younger sisters—Rachelle, who was thirteen, and Morgan, who was eleven. Her father worked for the government. Her mother worked for the Bureau of Indian

Affairs, and her mother was Native American, which explained Nikki's pretty, almond-shaped eyes, high cheekbones, and golden skin.

Tara, on the other hand, had been less forthcoming. She'd admitted to having no parents except for Uncle Pat, and that they moved around a lot. The rest she left unsaid.

"Well, thanks for the ride," Tara said as she reached for the door handle.

"No. Thank *you* for Corey," Nikki said.

Tara smiled. "Yeah. Sure."

"So . . . see you tomorrow?"

Tara's smile widened. "Okay."

For a day that had started out weird and moved into stressful, it was ending on a high note. Tara waved as Nikki drove away, and when she went into the house, her steps were bouncing.

She didn't sense DeeDee anywhere around, which, considering the day she'd had, was good.

She changed into a pair of shorts and traded tennis shoes for flip-flops, then got out her homework and dug in. An hour into it, she stopped long enough to make a casserole of baked beans and wieners and pop it in the oven, then went back to work. She was finishing the last of it when the timer went off, signaling the casserole was done.

Tara shoved her books and paper aside and got up to get a couple of potholders from the drawer. She set the casserole aside to cool, and began making a salad when she heard a car drive up. She glanced at the clock then frowned. It was early for Uncle Pat.

When the doorbell rang, she put the salad in the fridge to stay cool and was wiping her hands when Henry popped up in front of her, waving his hands in a panic.

"What?" Tara asked.

Don't open the door.

Startled by their warnings, Tara's heart thumped erratically. "Why? Who's out there?" she asked, and slipped into the living room to peek out the window. Curiosity was replaced by shock and then fear.

Emmit Broyles!

He'd run her off his property and now he was here? What could he possibly have to say to her that was good? He'd already denied having a sister, and at the mention of ghosts, he turned as pale as one. Tara didn't have to be told by her own two ghosts not to let him in. "Hello! Anybody home?" Emmit Broyles yelled, and then knocked loudly on the door again.

Tara flinched, but stood still, waiting for him to leave.

Only he didn't.

To Tara's horror, the doorknob turned. Then she heard keys jangling and gasped in shock. Surely he didn't still have a key to the place? Surely someone had changed the locks years ago?

When she heard a key slipping into the lock, she bolted down the hall. She started to hide in her room, then something told her to run to Uncle Pat's instead. She jumped into his closet, crawled behind his clothes, then pulled them all in front of her until she was completely hidden. All she could think about was her cell phone, lying on the kitchen table beside her homework. Emmit was bound to figure out someone was home.

Then her heart nearly stopped.

Maybe that was his intention all along. Maybe he'd come at this time on purpose, knowing she'd be here alone. Maybe he was intending to kill her.

Oh God, oh God, please don't let him find me.

Then she heard him in their house.

His footsteps were loud on the wooden floors as he moved through the rooms. She guessed he was following his nose first, because she heard him go into the kitchen, but he didn't stay there long. She heard doors opening, then closing in the living room, and knew he'd looked in both closets. Then she heard him coming down the hall. Her heart was beating so hard and so loud she could hardly breathe. She clamped her hands over her mouth to keep from screaming and closed her eyes, willing him to leave.

Footsteps stopped in the hall outside the door to Uncle Pat's room, then, just as she'd guessed, he went straight into her room. She heard him opening drawers and doors and cringed, imagining him putting his huge, ugly hands all over her things, handling her underwear, shuffling through the hangars where she'd hung her clothes. Looking in her bathroom, touching her things.

OMG, this could not be happening.

Then it got worse. She heard him exit her bedroom and pause, then he opened the door to Uncle Pat's room.

Oh please, oh please, oh please, Tara prayed.

His footsteps were less firm here, and she realized he'd stepped up on the braided rug at the foot of Uncle Pat's bed. Obviously, he knew this was a man's room. Everything in it, including the old shoes shoved beneath the old rocking chair were made for a man.

She didn't move and was barely breathing when she heard him open the door to the closet. She felt rather than saw the first hangars moving aside, then all of a sudden, she heard him scream. It was a high-pitched sound, almost like a girl.

She didn't know what had happened, but he was running and the sounds were fading, which meant he was moving away from her. She heard the front door open, then slam shut, then the sound of a car engine starting. Emmit Broyles gunned the engine of his car and left rubber on their driveway, then more rubber on the street in front of their house.

Tara was shaking when she finally got up and crawled out.

She sat down on the side of Uncle Pat's bed and tried to quit trembling, but the longer she sat, the worse it got until she found herself sobbing.

Suddenly, she realized she was no longer alone. Only it wasn't Henry and Millicent that she sensed. She looked up, and then shuddered on a sob.

DeeDee.

It was DeeDee, and there was a look of anger on her face. Understanding hit like a fist in the stomach. Now she knew what had made Emmit Broyles scream like a girl. He'd just seen his sister's ghost.

"Was it you?" Tara asked, then heard DeeDee sigh. "I think you just saved my life," she added.

DeeDee drifted toward her, but this time Tara felt no threat.

"Did he kill you? Was it your brother who buried your body in the back yard?"

No answer. Tara frowned. Millicent had been right. DeeDee truly didn't know.

"What can you tell me about where you were buried?"

A brief image of upturned earth and a pile of leaves flashed through Tara's mind and then it was gone—along with DeeDee.

That's when Tara realized she was hearing another car pull up into the driveway. She glanced at the clock. That would be Uncle Pat.

She debated about telling him what had happened, then knew if she told, she would also have to confess to visiting Emmit Broyles first, and that would lead to admitting she'd seen DeeDee's ghost, and then telling him there was a body buried in the back yard and the reason she knew it was there was because Millicent told her, and then having to explain that Millicent was her own personal ghost, which would send Uncle Pat into a frenzy. He'd solve all this by moving again before she could say no, and she didn't want to leave. For the first time in her life, Tara felt like this place might actually become their first home. Not just another place to rent on their way to somewhere else.

All she had to do was find DeeDee's body, and get the ball rolling on an investigation that would take Emmit Broyles out of polite society for keeps. So when she heard the front door open, she bolted out of his room and then headed down the hall to meet Uncle Pat with a smile on her face and a spring in her step, as if her day had been just about perfect. If her act had been filmed, she would have been nominated for an Oscar.

"Hey, Tara, honey. Something sure smells good," Uncle Pat said, as he gave her a hug.

"Baked beans and weenies. Your favorite."

"Boy, oh boy. Let me change and wash up and I'll be right there."

He gave her a quick kiss and then went to his room as Tara staggered into the kitchen. She put away her homework and then set the table. By the time he came in, she'd pulled herself together.

The evening passed without further consequence, although Tara made a decision to convince Uncle Pat he needed to change the locks on the house, and to get herself a weapon. Even though she seriously doubted Emmit Broyles would have the guts to come back and face his sister's ghost again, she wasn't taking any chances.

Chapter Six

It wasn't until Tara got to school the next day that she learned her lunatic life was about to get worse. Besides the ongoing drama of high school, a new and frightening fact had been added.

Bethany Fanning was missing.

According to those in the know, Bethany had called her father after cheerleading practice yesterday, said she was stopping at the supermarket then coming straight home. Only she never arrived.

After hours of worry and calling her cell phone with no answer, her parents found her car abandoned in the supermarket parking lot. The car wouldn't start, although the keys were still in the ignition. The police first supposed that she'd probably started to walk home after experiencing car trouble, only that didn't hold water. She would have called her father to come get her. And her purse was still in the car, lying on the floor. Her cell phone was on the seat, as if she'd tossed it inside then disappeared.

Tara was as stunned by the news as everyone else, but it wasn't until the police showed up at school and began calling students out of class that it became clear they were questioning all of Bethany's friends about her last hours on campus. The heck of it was, when they were through with her friends, they were bound to start with her enemies, and Tara was willing to bet that her name would be on that list.

When the bell rang for lunch, Tara put her backpack in her locker then headed for the lunchroom. She went through the line, choosing a hamburger and fries. She was reaching for fruit and cookies when someone slid their tray into hers.

She looked up. It was Nikki Scott, and she was smiling.

"Hey," Nikki said.

The friendly smile was not only welcome, it was slightly surprising. Tara hadn't really expected Nikki to acknowledge her again.

"Hey, yourself," Tara said.

"You sittin' with anyone?" Nikki asked.

"No."

"Come sit with us," Nikki said, then led the way to a table where a couple of other kids were already parked. "Hey guys," Nikki said, as she slid her tray on the table. "This is Tara. Tara, these are my friends, Mackenzie and Penny."

"Hi," Tara said.

"Hi yourself," Mackenzie said. "Just call me Mac."

Penny scooted over to give Tara room to sit.

Overwhelmed by the unexpected gesture, Tara gladly slid into the seat.

"Cool, what you did," Mac said. "Helping Corey like that."

"Yeah. Seriously cool," Penny added, then pointed to Nikki's plate. "You gonna eat that pickle?"

Nikki frowned as she covered her plate with her hands. "Dang, Penny. I just sat down. And yes, I'm going to eat my pickle. I love dill pickles. Why else would I put them on my plate?"

"To give to me?" Penny said, and then grinned.

Everyone laughed, and the meal began. Bethany's disappearance was a key topic, but no one could believe anything serious had happened to her. "Probably hooked up with some guy," Penny said.

Tara answered questions between bites, and asked a few of her own. By the time they were finished, she knew that the girls were on the high school softball team, and that Nikki was a star pitcher. A fact Nikki had neglected to mention yesterday.

Finally, there was a lull in the banter.

"So how is Corey today?" Tara asked.

"He's good," Nikki said. "Except his folks are taking him to Tulsa to run some tests tomorrow. Something about his heart rhythm."

Tara nodded. "That's good. I hope the doctors figure out what's wrong and make him better."

"You and me, both," Nikki said.

Mac licked the ketchup from a finger, then angled a look up at Tara. "So, what's your thing?" she asked.

Tara frowned. "My thing?"

"Yeah. You know. Sports. Art. Debate. Choir. Your thing? What's your fav?"

Well, well, Millicent inserted. *Is it me, or Henry?*

Tara grinned. Millicent was always claiming to be Tara's favorite. *Wouldn't you just love to know,* she thought.

"Growing up, we've moved around so much that it never paid to get involved. I'm no good at sports. I tried band one year. Uncle Pat rented my instrument... a clarinet... and before I got past the first few lessons, we'd moved. After that, I never bothered again."

"No biggie," Mac said. "So, who's the Hollywood hottie who winds up in your dreams?"

Tara grinned. "I'm liking me some Orlando Bloom."

"He's so old!"

"How about Taylor Lautner?"

"The guy who plays the werewolf?"

"Oooh, sister. That's what I'm talking about," Nikki said, and then high-fived Tara.

They laughed in unison, which drew a few stares from kids at nearby tables, before they looked away. Mel and Prissy gave Tara such scalding looks that her skin prickled. *They're up to something.*

When her last class of the day rolled around, Tara had barely been seated before her name was called over the loudspeaker.

"Tara Luna. Report to the principal's office."

Tara's heart skipped a beat.

Her teacher nodded, giving her permission to leave, and Tara gathered up her stuff and left the classroom without looking back. She imagined everyone, including Flynn, whispering among themselves as to what was about to happen, picturing her hauled away in handcuffs.

Her feet were dragging as she started up the hall. She hadn't spoken to Mrs. Crabtree since yesterday's incident. Facing her *and* the police was going to be tricky.

I'm with you all the way.

"For God's sake . . . and mine, Millicent. Whatever you do, don't help."

Whatever.

Tara sighed. That's all she needed. Flying coffee cups and airborne pencils. A few moments later, she reached the office, then knocked on the door.

"Come in."

Tara walked inside, closing the door behind her. Besides Mrs. Crabtree, there were three other people in the room. Two were detectives. She saw the badges clipped to their belts. All of a sudden, her psychic sense kicked in. The third man was the school attorney. So, if the school needed a lawyer, then where was hers?

I'm here if you need me.

No, Millicent. For the last time, let me handle this.

"Tara, this is Detective Rutherford and Detective Allen of the Stillwater police. The gentleman to my right is Walker Mowbry, attorney for Stillwater Public Schools. Gentlemen, this is Tara Luna. She's a new student in our senior class."

"Hi guys," Tara said, and shifted her backpack. "Am I sitting down, or do I line up against the wall and wait for the firing squad?"

Detective Rutherford grinned. Detective Allen looked away. The attorney frowned. Mrs. Crabtree knew better than to comment. She was still trying to come to terms with the fact that this strange girl, who claimed to be psychic, had correctly predicted she would find money in two places in her home. She and her husband had stayed up until after midnight last night counting it. It was something over seventy-eight thousand dollars, including the bills that the mice had been nibbling on. She didn't know whether to thank this young woman or wear a necklace of garlic bulbs around her neck.

"Have a seat, dear," she said.

"Garlic is for vampires, not witches," Tara whispered, then propped her backpack against the chair, sat down and waited. Mrs. Crabtree moaned, and sank back into her chair.

Detective Rutherford frowned at the her and Tara, then took out a small notepad and flipped it open while the other detective moved into her line of sight and sat on the corner of the principal's desk.

"As you know, we're investigating the disappearance of one of your classmates, Bethany Fanning," Detective Allen said.

Tara nodded.

"Can you tell us about your day yesterday? I understand you had a run-in with Bethany."

Tara frowned. "Um . . . no sir, that's not true. I've hardly spoken a half-dozen words to her since the year started. It's her friend, Prissy, who's decided I don't deserve to draw breath."

"Really?" he drawled, then glanced down at his notebook.

Tara could see the words as clearly as if she was reading them herself, even though he was across the room from her.

"No I am not a wiccan. A witch. A wizard. None of the above."

Allen looked startled, then glanced up at Tara. "Er . . . you say you did not argue with Bethany?"

"No sir. Bethany is kind of stuck on herself, but she seems okay. She just hangs out with a psycho named Prissy."

"Are you referring to Priscilla Marshall?"

"Is that her name? All I know is Prissy."

"Why did you call Prissy a psycho?"

"Where do I start? She cheated on a test and got caught and blames me. She got kicked off the cheerleading squad and somehow that's my fault, too. And it's all because I don't bow down when I see her. She's spread it all over school that I'm a witch. Look at me. A witch? I mean . . . she's a psycho, okay?"

"Is this true, Mrs. Crabtree?"

Tara glanced over at the principal, who looked at her

nervously, then looked away.

"The facts Tara stated *are* true. Priscilla likes to cause trouble."

"Hmm," Detective Rutherford said, and then he began asking questions while Allen stepped aside. "So, where did you go after school yesterday?"

"Home."

"Can anyone vouch for that?"

"One of the janitors saw me in the hall after most of the others were gone. I waved at him as I left."

"What's the janitor's name?"

"I don't' know. He's the tall skinny one with red hair."

"That would be Harold Wells," the principal said.

The detective made a note.

Tara continued. "As I was leaving, a girl named Nikki Scott met me on the steps outside and gave me a ride home. Otherwise I would have walked."

"You don't own a car?"

"No. My Uncle Pat and I share one."

"Where are your parents?"

"I don't have any. They died when I was a baby. There's just Uncle Pat and me."

"Is he home?"

"No sir. He's a meter reader for the city of Stillwater. His name is Patrick Carmichael." She recited his cell phone number. The detective made some more notes.

"Who's Nikki Scott to you? Does she give you a ride every day?"

"No sir. I didn't know her until yesterday."

"It's quite a coincidence that you suddenly have an alibi for your whereabouts yesterday, when you wouldn't have had before."

Tara didn't like the tone of his voice, and she knew Millicent didn't either.

"People don't wake up thinking to give themselves an alibi for every day of their life. At least I don't. And the reason I just met Nikki Scott yesterday is because, on that same day, she claims I saved her boyfriend's life and she came back to thank me."

Now all three men were paying attention. Mrs. Crabtree looked nervous. She'd forgotten to mention that, earlier. Now she feared it would appear she'd been trying to influence the detectives against Tara.

"Is that so?" Rutherford asked. "How did you do that?"

Tara glared at the principal. "Mrs. Crabtree knows. I would have thought she'd told you."

"Well. I'm sorry. That incident completely slipped my mind after learning of Bethany's disappearance."

Tara looked calmly at the detectives. "A kid named Corey Palmer was having a seizure on the floor of the boy's bathroom yesterday afternoon. I called for help. Coach Jones performed CPR, brought him back to life, and I understand he's okay today. Nikki Scott goes with Corey Palmer, only I didn't know either one of them until yesterday because I'm new. It seems that makes me the favorite butt to kick. I'm really sorry Bethany Fanning is missing, but I don't hang out with her and don't see her outside of school. So that's how I got my ride home with Nikki Scott, which has turned out lucky for me because it seems I need an alibi, and that's where I was the rest of the evening . . . with Uncle Pat . . . eating beans and weenies and doing homework until after 11:00, because I think Mrs. Farmer must like to grade papers."

Detective Allen stifled a smile.

"Thank you, Miss Luna. I believe that's all we need from you for now," he said.

"Yes, sir." Then she added. "I hope you find Bethany soon." Then she reached down to pick up her backpack.

As she did, the pen Detective Rutherford was holding exploded. Allen took a step back and then fell because his shoelaces were tied together. Mrs. Crabtree screamed and dived under her desk.

Tara sighed.

"I told you not to do that," she muttered to Millicent, as she headed for the door.

"What the hell just happened?" the lawyer yelled.

She heard Mrs. Crabtree whimpering.

Tara shouldered her backpack and kept on moving.

No one messes with my girl, Millicent said.

Tara grinned all the way back to class. As she opened the door, everyone, including Flynn, looked up.

The teacher acknowledged her with a nod, and Tara returned to her seat. It wasn't five minutes before the intercom sounded in their room again. "Flynn O'Mara, please report to the principal's office."

Tara heard Flynn shuffling papers and books behind her, but she didn't even look up as he passed by her desk. She didn't know how she felt about him anymore, but she didn't wish him any harm.

The bell rang before he came back, so Tara didn't have the opportunity to pick up on his emotions to see how it went. Which, she reminded herself, was just as well. He'd already disappointed her once. No need setting herself up for another fall.

Outside the school building, a group had assembled. As Tara came closer, she realized it was members of the cheerleading squad and pep squad, as well as several of the football players. They had a clipboard, trying to get kids to sign up to help with a car wash to help raise money to add to the reward her parents had already posted. Fifty thousand dollars was a bunch of money. If someone had seen anything suspicious, they would surely come forward with the information.

As she passed by the group, Mel caught Tara's eye, hesitated, then walked toward her.

"Um . . . hey . . . lunatic, I mean, Tara . . . would you like to help with the car wash this Saturday?"

Once more, Tara was surprised by the offer. "Yeah, sure. Where are you having it, and what time?"

"The parking lot of Stillwater National Bank. That's where Bethany's father works. And we're having it from 9:00 a.m. until 5:00. Just sign your name on the hour or hours you can help. We would appreciate it."

Tara noticed that most of the afternoon hours were already taken, which meant no one wanted to wake up early on Saturday. Considering all that had passed between her and the trio of cheerleaders, she figured she could wake up a little early for a good cause. She signed herself up from 9 to 11.

"I hope they find Bethany before Saturday," Tara said, as she handed the clipboard back to Mel.

Mel nodded, then watched as Tara walked away.

Tara had planned to spend some time in the backyard searching for DeeDee's grave again. She wasn't too worried about Emmit Broyles making a return trip to their house. Not after seeing his dead sister's ghost. Still, she needed to resolve the issue and finding the body was the only thing that would start an investigation into DeeDee's death.

But the sky started darkening on her way home from school, and from the looks of the clouds, it was definitely going to rain. Not wanting to get caught out in another late summer thunderstorm, she began to walk faster. About four blocks from home, she heard the first rumblings of thunder.

Better run for it.

"Shoot," Tara said, but she knew Millicent's warnings well enough to heed them.

She shifted her backpack to a more secure location and started running, and it was a good thing she did. The first drops of rain were just beginning to fall when she hit the front porch steps. Now that she was safely under the porch, she quickly unlocked the door and hurried inside. The rain was coming down in sheets, and the wind had started to blow. She switched on the TV to see if they were under any weather alerts. Storms were one thing. Tornadoes were another. To her relief, it was just a fast-moving thunderstorm that was predicted to pass before nightfall. But it ended her plan to search the backyard again.

She made a quick run through the house, making sure all

the windows were shut. Once she was satisfied all was well, she grabbed a can of pop and a couple of cookies and began working on homework. The intermittent weather reports kept breaking into regular programming. She kept the sound turned down low, but the background noise was somehow comforting.

When a particularly loud roll of thunder sounded overhead, followed by a close lightning strike, it made her jump. She winced, then looked up and out at the downpour and wondered where Bethany was, and if she was even still alive. It was a horrible thought, but the world was not kind a one, especially to kids. Predators were everywhere.

It had occurred to her more than once to try and get a "fix" on Bethany, but psychically, nothing came through. Neither Henry or Millicent had mentioned her, which wasn't all that unusual. They didn't usually bother Tara with information from their world, unless it directly affected her or Uncle Pat.

A few minutes later, the phone rang. Tara got up to answer. It didn't occur to her until she was already putting the phone to her ear that Uncle Pat would have called her on her cell.

"Hello?"

"You bitch! What have you done with Bethany?"

Tara sighed. Prissy. "You know good and well I didn't do anything to her," Tara said calmly. "You're just scared and upset because your friend is missing. I get that. But you need to stop telling lies about me. I'm not going to put up with it forever."

"What? What are you going to do? Make me disappear, too?"

"Do you hear yourself?" Tara said. "Make you disappear? Are you nuts? I am no freakin' witch or magician, here. I don't make my classmates do disappearing acts."

"Then how do you explain that dust devil? And food flying through the air in the lunch room, and the stuff you know about us that you shouldn't know?"

"I don't explain myself, Prissy. I try to mind my own

business. You really need to do the same."

Tara hung up.

She sighed in frustration and started to return to her homework when an image flashed through her mind so fast she almost thought she'd imagined it. It was Bethany locked in a closet. She held a half-eaten bag of cheese puffs and a bottle of soda near her feet. And she was crying. Then it was gone.

Tara turned in a circle, trying to decide what to do first. Should she call the police? Should she . . .

What do you plan to say to the police? That you had a vision?

Tara stopped. Her shoulders slumped, then she exhaled slowly as reality surfaced.

"Yeah. Right. What do I say? Oh . . . say guys . . . you might like to know I just saw Bethany Fanning. No . . . not in person. Just in my head. No, sorry, I don't know where she is or who has her. All I know is she's alive and tied up like a Thanksgiving turkey."

She sat down at the kitchen table. "This sucks," she said, then folded her arms on the table and buried her head.

It's not your job to save the world.

Tara lifted her head. The rain was still coming down. The television was still playing. Nothing had changed—except that Tara knew something no one else in the world knew—that someone had kidnapped Bethany—and she couldn't do anything about it.

"If it's not my job, then why do I see what I see, if I'm not supposed to make a difference?"

Henry popped up in front of the window. Tara sighed. How weird was it to watch it rain through the belly of a ghost?

"I don't suppose you have anything to tell me about Bethany?" He raised his hands in a helpless gesture. "Thanks anyway."

Before she could ask him anything else, there was a knock on her door. The last time someone had knocked at the door, it had been Emmit. She grabbed her cell phone as she headed into the living room. If it was Broyles, she wasn't going to be caught without a way to call for help again.

She didn't see a car when she looked out the window, then she peered sideways and gasped. Flynn? Should she let him in? He knocked again.

Oh for pity's sake. I'll do it.

Before Tara could stop her, Millicent opened the door. The fact that Tara was a good fifteen feet away from the door handle was not lost on Flynn as he stared at her standing in the living room.

"What the hell?" he muttered.

"Don't ask," Tara said, as she hurried forward. "Oh my gosh . . . you're soaked. What were you thinking, coming all this way in the rain?"

Flynn sighed. "I was thinking I didn't want to spend another night feeling guilty for hurting your feelings."

Tara's heart skipped a beat. How sweet is this?

Don't gush all over him. Play hard to get.

Mind your own business, Tara thought. "So come in out of the rain," she said.

He shook his head. "No. I'll get everything all wet. I just wanted to stop by and tell you I'm sorry. I'm sorry. I'm sorry."

Tara wanted to throw her arms around his neck and hug him madly.

"I'm glad you stopped by," she said.

Flynn combed his wet hair away from his face with his fingers, then nodded.

"So . . . that's that," he said, and started to leave.

"Wait!" Tara said.

"Yeah?"

"You got grilled by the police today, too, didn't you?"

"Oh yeah. Did they ask if you had an alibi for yesterday afternoon, too?"

"Yes. Luckily, Nikki Scott had given me a ride home. I can't believe they think one of us would hurt Bethany. What did you tell them?"

"I was bussing tables at Eskimo Joe's until almost midnight. Mom and I rode home together."

"Lucky for you."

"Yeah. Uh . . . Bethany and I sort of . . . uh, this past summer she—"

"Oh, I know all about that, including the fact that she didn't dump you. You're the one who called it off. She was using you to tick off her parents, wasn't she? Stupid move. Hope it didn't hurt your feelings."

Flynn was stunned, and it showed. "How do you know all that? I didn't tell anyone, and I can guarantee Bethany wouldn't own up to it."

Tara shrugged, then smiled. "I just know stuff, okay? So, did you tell the police? You should have."

"I told them, all right," he said. "But they didn't believe me. They couldn't believe that a guy like me would turn down a babe like Bethany. I'm supposed to be too young to be selective."

"Sorry."

"It's not your problem," he said.

"It might be. I mean . . . I'm still the dangerous witch of Stillwater High. Who knows what lies that psycho Prissy is going to be spreading next?"

"Yeah. So . . . we're all right now? I mean, you're not mad at me anymore for—"

"We're totally all right," Tara said, and then lifted her hand for him to give her a high-five. Instead, he took her hand and pulled her forward just far enough to give her a quick kiss.

"See you tomorrow," he said. "Stay dry." He headed back out in the rain, running in a long, steady lope.

Tara's heart was pounding and her lips were still tingling as she watched him leave. She stood until he turned a corner and ran out of sight. She was just about to go back into the house when she saw Uncle Pat's car coming down the street, so she waited, watching as he pulled up into the driveway, then jumped out on the run, and vaulted up on the porch.

"Wow. It's really coming down, isn't it, honey?" he said, as he gave her a quick kiss.

"Yes, really coming down," she echoed, and followed him inside.

Chapter Seven

Fear was so thick in her throat she couldn't swallow. . . I want to go home. Please just let me go home. I won't tell. I promise. Just let me go.

Shut up. Just shut up. I can't think when you keep talking like that.

She hiccupped in fear but did as he said. He hadn't hurt her yet, but he looked like he might. Everyone knew there was something wrong with him. Sometimes he cried when she cried, and he kept saying he was sorry, but he wouldn't let her go. She could hear him pacing from the end of the bed to the window and back again. Her heart skipped a beat. Were the police out there? Had they finally found me? Please let them find me. I won't ever be selfish or mean again, I swear. I swear.

"Please, let me out. I want to go home," she yelled.

Suddenly, the door flew back and he was looming in the doorway.

"It's all your fault. If you'd just listened instead of laughing at me. Everyone laughs at me."

He slammed the door shut again, and locked it.

Tara sat straight up in bed, her heart pounding so hard she couldn't hear herself breathe.

Did I just dream about Bethany being bullied by a psycho kidnapper or what?

She looked at the clock. It was just past four in the morning. Rain was still dripping from the eaves of the house, although most of the thunderstorm had passed. She swung her legs over to the side of the bed then got up. No way was she going back to sleep now. Besides, she needed to think about what she'd been dreaming.

It was weird, but in the dream, she had been in Bethany's body, feeling her fear, her hunger, even her pain. And the guy who was holding Bethany hostage. Tara shuddered. She scrubbed her hands across her face in frustration, wanting answers that wouldn't come. What had he looked like? In the dream she'd only seen him from the back. Even more to the point, was that just a dream, or did she just have another vision?

Tara tiptoed out of her bedroom and then down the hall to the bathroom. When she came out, she headed for the kitchen. *Just a dream*, she told herself. *Drown it in chocolate.* Might as well see if Uncle Pat had left any of that cake from the supermarket bakery.

And he had.

She cut a piece of chocolate cake, then poured herself a glass of milk and settled down at the table. There was an odd sort of comfort in being awake at this time of morning. Like the calm after a storm. The cake was sweet. The milk was cold. *Everyone laughs at me.*

Tara gasped, almost choking on the cake. "Millicent. You scared me half to death."

I'm just reminding you of what he said in the dream.

Tara frowned. "I heard him. So what does that tell me? Everyone laughs at me, too, but I don't go around kidnaping people."

Think about it and you'll know.

"What kind of answer is that?"

Unfortunately, Millicent had said all she had to say on the subject. She disappeared.

Tara frowned as she took another bite of cake. What kinds of kids get laughed at? Fat kids. Skinny kids. Kids with big ears. Kids with bad skin. Kids who are into Goth. Kids who aren't into Goth. Anybody who doesn't fit in gets laughed at. This was no help at all.

Still, as she finished her cake and milk then took the dirty dishes to the sink, she made a conscious decision to pay attention at school. See if anyone there seemed seriously certifiable.

She gathered up her homework from last night and

slipped it all into her backpack, folded a load of towels from the dryer, then decided to make Uncle Pat his favorite breakfast. She glanced at the clock. It was almost five. He had to be at work by seven, so he would be up within the hour.

She started the coffee, dug through the fridge for a can of refrigerated biscuits, pulled out the sausage links and a jug of milk and got busy. When five-thirty rolled around, she had biscuits coming out of the oven and sausage and gravy cooked and warming on the stove. Obviously the aroma of her early morning endeavors had done the job. She could hear Uncle Pat's footsteps coming down the hall.

"My goodness!" he said, as he entered the kitchen. "Am I dreaming?"

"Grab a plate and see if it tastes as good as it smells."

"Yum," he said, and gave her a good morning hug. "You're the best, honey. The absolute best."

The praise lifted her spirits, which were in sad need of lifting. She hadn't told him about being questioned by the police, because then she would have had to explain about the hassles she'd been enduring. She had given the detectives Uncle Pat's name and phone number, but didn't think they'd done any more than verify her information, because he hadn't asked her about it. It was crazy, Bethany being missing and all, but it wasn't her fault. No need bothering Uncle Pat with something he couldn't fix.

Just watching his face and seeing the delight a simple breakfast had brought was enough to get Tara through the day. He soon left for work, leaving Tara to clean up the kitchen, then get ready for school. A short while later, she was in her room, trying to pick out something to wear. According to the weatherman, it might rain again today, which meant needing to take some kind of jacket.

She pulled on a pair of her newer jeans, then stood in front of the mirror, eyeing the wide legs and low ride on her hips, then decided to tuck in her red tee and add a funky belt.

"Not bad for a skinny girl," Tara muttered, as she turned first one way, then another, making sure she was tucked and zipped in all the right places.

She'd already done her hair, pulling the sides away from her face, then fastening it at the back of her head with a wide, tortoise shell clip, letting the rest of it fall free. She slathered on a pale lip gloss, then squinted her eyes until she could almost see a resemblance to Angelina Jolie. That's when she knew she was ready.

Looking like a hottie, chica.

"Dang, Millicent . . . where have you been . . . in Mexico? What's with the *chica* business?"

Henry popped up in the mirror behind her long enough to give her what amounted to a virtual hug, then vaporized.

Tara sighed. No one would believe her life, even if she tried to tell it. Talk about crazy.

She grabbed her jacket and her backpack and headed for the door. She got to school only to find Flynn waiting for her at the front door. She was so surprised that she actually stumbled, which made her feel like a goof. But having him to walk down the hall with her was worth it.

The rest of the week passed quickly. Bethany was still missing. Tara tried with all her might to lock into Bethany's head again, but it didn't work.

Prissy gave her 'go to hell' looks every time she saw her, but didn't seem willing to confront her anymore. Obviously, Millicent's stunt with the dust devil had done some good after all.

Nikki Scott, Mac and Penny were still being friendly—a gesture Tara definitely appreciated—while Flynn spent every school day upping the heater meter on staking a claim. Besides walking her to classes, sometimes he joined her and her new BFFs in the lunchroom. And every day that he didn't have to work at Eskimo Joe's after school, he walked her home. Tara was beginning to feel like a normal girl.

It was a mistake she'd made before and would most likely make again, but for now, it felt amazing. If she could just figure out where DeeDee was buried and find Bethany, her life would be just about perfect.

Then Saturday rolled around. The day for the car wash.

Tara was out of bed and on her way downtown to the bank by 8:30, determined not to be late. Everywhere she drove, she saw hundreds of yellow ribbons tied all over the trees in town. And there were flyers about Bethany stapled to trees and fences and power poles, anywhere a staple could be driven, a flyer went up.

I want to help. Why can't I tune in to Bethany's thoughts?

She was sick at heart that the bits and pieces she'd 'seen' about Bethany's situation weren't enough to take to the police.

When Tara drove up to the bank, the first people she saw were Bethany's parents. They were standing hand in hand, thanking the students for doing this. They'd brought several boxes of doughnuts and cartons of fruit juice, and Bethany's mother couldn't pass more than five or ten minutes without crying. It was the first time Tara had been face to face with the depth of their despair, and felt even more guilt that she hadn't been able to reconnect.

She wondered what would happen if she could get closer to them—maybe pick up on something that would link her to Bethany—but they hustled into their car and left. She threw herself into the car wash with all the enthusiasm she could muster, washing, drying, polishing a continuous line of vehicles.

It was a little bit after ten when she looked up and realized Flynn was there. He was squatting down beside a big yellow Hummer, polishing the chrome rims. Tara couldn't help but wonder how much it cost to fill that monster ride with gas, then glanced back at Flynn. He'd shed his t-shirt and tucked it through a belt loop on the back of his jeans. His skin was an all-over brown, making that skull and barbed wire tattoo he'd gotten over the summer shine like a new penny.

Nice tush.

Tara jumped. She'd been thinking what Millicent just said.

So, are you going to go talk to him, or just stand and wait for him to bend a little farther over in hopes that his tidy whities show?

Millicent! You are so bad.

Tara heard what sounded like a ghostly snort, then felt Millicent zap out.

At that point, Flynn stood up and turned around. When he saw Tara a wide smile broke across his face as he waved.

Her heart skipped a beat. Dang. He looked as good from the front as he did from behind. Talk about a six-pack belly. He was ripped. She tossed her sponge into a bucket of water and started to go over when Davis Breedlove suddenly walked out of a crowd of guys and headed toward Flynn.

Tara felt Davis's frustration and fear and knew this wasn't going to be good.

Davis walked straight up to Flynn and began poking him in the chest with his finger, well aware he would be asking for a fight.

"What the hell are you doing here? Gloating?" Davis said.

Shock spread across Flynn's face, followed by a rush of anger. "Back off," he said. "I'm just washing cars here, okay?"

"No. It's not okay," Davis shouted. "You had something to do with Bethany going missing. The cops can't prove it, but they know it."

"You're crazy!" Flynn muttered. "They know where I was . . . at work with my Mom."

"Oh. Your Mother the barfly?"

OMG. He did not just say that, Tara thought.

Flynn's first punch hit Davis on the chin. It sent him staggering, but he came back with a roar of rage and hit Flynn in the belly.

There was a moment of stunned silence, and then everyone began shouting. Tara was in a panic. When she heard someone talking about calling the cops, she knew she had to act. She grabbed a hose and turned it on full blast, dousing both Davis and Flynn in the face until they were both forced to back off just to breathe.

Then she dropped the hose, grabbed Flynn by the arm, and began dragging him toward her car. He had a cut over his eye, a cut on his cheek and a busted lip. Davis didn't look any better, but because he was Bethany's boyfriend, the crowd's sympathy was with him.

"Let me go," Flynn muttered, as Tara kept pulling him along.

"Just shut up and get in," she said as she opened the car door and shoved him into the passenger side.

Then she circled the car on the run and slid behind the wheel. For once, the engine turned over on the first try. In the distance, she could hear the sounds of sirens. Crap. Someone had called the cops. She left rubber on the concrete as she peeled out of the parking lot and didn't look back.

Take a left at the next street.

Tara didn't question Millicent's directions. She just did as she was told. A few moments later she heard the sirens getting closer. She glanced up into the rearview mirror, then saw them go sailing past in the street behind her.

Thank you, Millicent.

I take care of my clucks.

Peeps, it's peeps—but thank you anyway. She glanced back up at the rearview mirror again, then jumped in reflex. Henry was looking back with a worried expression on his face.

"It's all good," Tara said. Henry nodded, then vaporized.

Flynn thought she was talking to him and frowned. "Nothing is good," he said.

Tara glanced over briefly. Blood was running from his nose down onto his chest.

"You're bleeding," she said, and handed him his t-shirt, which he'd tossed onto the seat between them.

He stuffed it up against his nose and then leaned back, trying to stop the blood flow.

"Just take me home," he muttered.

"I think you need stitches in your cheek."

"No stitches. No doctors. Just take me home."

"And that would be where?"

"Oh. Right." He raised up long enough to see where they were. "Um . . . turn left at the apartment buildings on the next block."

Tara knew he was angry and embarrassed. His feelings

were hurt by what Davis Breedlove had accused him of, but even angrier at what he'd called Flynn's mother.

"Your mother is great," Tara said. "Anyone who's ever been in Joe's knows what a nice lady she is . . . always smiling . . . always friendly."

"On the nights she doesn't work late at Joe's, she works at a bar."

Tara felt his anguish as clearly as if he was crying.

"Yeah, I know. She works hard to keep you guys afloat, doesn't she? That's sort of the way with Uncle Pat. He has all kinds of degrees, but he also has a gypsy soul. Just when I think we might settle in a place, he's off to bigger and better things. We're always scrambling to play catch up for the first couple of months after we move."

She felt Flynn's tension easing and glanced over at him again. "So, I just turned left. Where to now?"

Flynn sighed. "Go five blocks down, then turn right on North Lewis. It's the second house on the right."

"Will do," Tara said, and kept on driving.

Flynn didn't look at her. He'd already been humiliated enough for one day. Seeing disgust on her face would be the last straw. A couple of minutes later, he felt the car turning. He took the t-shirt off his nose long enough to look. They were in his driveway.

As soon as she put the car in park, he opened the door and got out. "Thanks for the ride," he said.

Only Tara didn't answer. When he looked back, she was getting out of the car.

"You don't have to—"

"You helped me, remember? Allow me the privilege of giving back."

Flynn sighed. "Fine. Whatever," he said, and led the way to the house.

"Is your Mom home?" Tara asked.

"No, she's at work."

"Where do you keep alcohol and Band-Aids?"

"Bathroom . . . down the hall."

"I'll be right back," Tara said.

Flynn dropped onto the sofa, then leaned back and closed his eyes. His face felt like he'd walked into a swinging ball bat and his feelings were hurt. He wished he'd never gone to that stupid car wash.

Tara quickly found what she was looking for, grabbed a wet washcloth, then headed back to the living room. Flynn was on the sofa. She felt his anguish clear across the room, but she couldn't let on. It would only make things worse.

"Lean back," she said, took the wet cloth and began cleaning up the blood.

"I can do that," Flynn said, and reached up.

"Put your hand down please, I can't see what I'm doing," Tara said, and proceeded to clean up the cuts. When she opened the alcohol, she warned him. "This is probably going to hurt."

"Just do it," Flynn said, then stifled a moan when the alcohol swabs hit the gashes on his cheek and over his eye.

"I'm so sorry," Tara said softly. "As soon as that dries, I'll put some Band-Aids on them. It's the best we can do, although I still say you need stitches, especially on your cheek."

A few minutes later, she was done. She carried the bloody washcloth to the bathroom and rinsed out as much blood as she could, then hung it back up to dry. His mother was going to freak when she saw it, though. She sighed. What a mixed up mess for everyone.

She hurried back into the living room, but Flynn wasn't there.

"Hey . . . where are you?"

"In here," he called.

She followed the sound of his voice into the kitchen and found him washing down some pain killers with a big drink of Pepsi.

"Your elbow is all skinned too," she said. "I missed that while ago."

He shrugged. "I've had worse for less reason."

"Will you be all right?"

It finally dawned on Flynn that Tara wasn't just being kind—that she was actually concerned.

"Yeah. Sure. And just for the record, thanks for getting me out of there before the cops came."

Tara nodded. "Sure . . . so . . . I guess I'd better go."

Flynn shoved his hands in his pockets as he looked at her from across the room. There was blood on the front of her t-shirt and her hair was down in her eyes. But she wasn't judging him, and she'd stepped up when everyone else wanted to put him down. She was about the prettiest thing he'd ever seen.

"Tara."

"Yes?"

"Thank you."

She sighed. "Yeah. Sure." Then she pointed toward the door. "I'd better be going now."

He nodded.

"Okay . . . bye," she said.

Flynn took his hands out of his pockets and walked toward her.

Tara knew before he touched her what he wanted. When he walked into her arms, she held him close, careful not to squeeze too tight.

For Flynn, it was like coming home. Safe and loving. He rested his cheek against the side of her head, feeling the softness of her hair against his face.

"You are something special," Flynn said. But when he tried to kiss her, it hurt the cut on his lip.

"Ow," he mumbled, and quickly pulled back.

"Poor baby," Tara said. "Here . . . we'll do it this way." She kissed the end of her own finger, then gently touched her finger to the corner of his mouth. "A totally painless make-out session."

Flynn groaned. Making out with Tara Luna would include way more than a kiss, but the relationship wasn't there yet, and if his luck continued to run as usual, it probably never would be.

Tara leaned back in his arms, letting her gaze roam over

her poor battered face. She couldn't resist, and touched the side of his cheek where the Band-Aid was.

"Don't say it again," he teased.

Tara grinned. "Stitches."

He laughed, then winced. "Go home, Moon girl. Drive safe and, once more, thanks for having my back."

"No prob," she said, and waved as she left.

She was backing out of the driveway when Henry popped up in the seat beside her, as if reminding her she wasn't alone.

I'm here, too.

"Of course you are," Tara said. "FYI, we're all going home now."

She accelerated down the street, heading for home, hoping Uncle Pat was in the back yard when she got there, because then she wouldn't have to lie to him about how she got the blood on her shirt.

As she drove, she kept thinking about the morning. Seeing Bethany's parents. Watching the faces of the seniors who'd slept soundly in their beds last night, secure in the knowledge that the world still revolved around them, then showing up on Bethany's behalf to have a car wash. Kind of pathetic in the grand scheme of things. But she understood the premise. They needed to help and that was the only thing they knew to do.

And then there's me, Tara thought. *I know stuff. Important stuff. But it's worthless unless I can find a way to prove it.* Flynn just got caught in the crossfire of everyone's fear and I have to find a way to fix this.

Tara was so focused on the missing cheerleader, she didn't notice the gray Lincoln behind her, unaware that it had been following her ever since she and Flynn had left the car wash, or that Emmit Broyles was behind the wheel.

But Millicent noticed.

Enemy at six o'clock.

Tara frowned as she looked up in the rearview mirror. Six o'clock would be right behind her. "What do you mean, enemy at . . . Crap! Is that Emmit Broyles?"

The tone of her voice shifted to a shriek, which sent

Henry into a tailspin. He vaporized right in front of her, causing her to slam on her brakes just before rear-ending the car in front of her.

I got this. Keep driving.

Tara gasped. She didn't take the time to argue. As soon as the light changed and the cars began to move, she hit the accelerator.

The gray Lincoln accelerated too. It was halfway through the intersection when Tara saw something she wouldn't have believed if she wasn't witnessing it with her own eyes.

The Lincoln was no longer moving, but Emmit was. He was crawling all over the inside of the car, trying to get out, but it appeared that the doors wouldn't open. Tara could see the panic on his face, but wasn't sure why. Then all of a sudden, a semi-truck came barreling through the intersection, sliding sideways and trying to miss the car that was stopped in the worst possible place. It clipped the bumper of Emmit Broyles car just enough to send it spinning.

Broyles mouth was wide open in fear. Somehow, what was happening seemed justified. Besides, who was she to interfere with the business of a pink-tinged wraith?

Tara had been home for a couple of hours before she found out where Uncle Pat had gone. He'd called her to tell her he was at Eskimo Joe's having lunch, and to see if she wanted him to bring her anything. Tara grinned when she heard his story and passed on the food. She'd already eaten lunch. But she knew her uncle hadn't just gone to Joe's to eat. He'd gone to see Mona, too.

How weird was this? She and Flynn. Uncle Pat and Flynn's Mom. Yikes.

She didn't know what to think about the fact that Emmit Broyles had been following her. There was no way that had been a coincidence. Not when Millicent had gone after him as she had. She wondered if Emmit was okay, then decided she didn't much care. Even though she couldn't prove it, the only reason Emmit would be trying to silence her was if he wanted his past deeds—and his younger sister—to stay buried.

Tara was in the driveway washing their aging Chevrolet Malibu when she saw Uncle Pat coming down the street. He waved. She waved back, then finished rinsing off the hood.

"Hey, thanks for washing the Chevy," Uncle Pat said, as he eyed his reflection in the blue metallic surface.

Tara smiled. "Started the day off washing cars. Decided I'd end it the same way."

"The day's not over and it's Saturday night. Surely you're not going to spend it sitting here with me?"

Tara thought of Flynn. He was probably too beat up to want to go out in public. That left her on her own, and after the latest run-in with Emmit, staying home was way safer than going out.

"I don't know. That sounds like a pretty good idea," Tara said, then narrowed her eyes and gave him a thoughtful look. "You're not trying to get rid of me or anything are you? Like . . . maybe you're planning on bringing your own company over tonight?"

The flush on her uncle's face was priceless. "Lord, no! What made you think of a thing like that?"

"Maybe because of where you had lunch."

"Lots of people eat there," he said.

Tara grinned. "I know . . . but I know you went because of Mona, not the food, and that's what made me think you might want the house to yourself."

He sputtered a bit, then frowned. "I'm sure I don't know what you mean. And, on another note, how was the car wash?"

Fine, until the fight. "Good. Good. I'm thinking we raised a lot of money to add to the reward for Bethany."

Uncle Pat sat down on the side of the porch, watching as Tara turned off the water and began drying off their car. She was the picture of her mother—brown eyes—slim and leggy with a heart-shaped face and a lot of thick, dark hair. And she was almost grown. Where had the years gone? He couldn't imagine what it would be like to know that she was missing.

"Do you know that missing girl? Do you know Bethany Fanning?" he asked.

"Oh. Sure I know who she is. I even have a class with her. But we don't hang. She's a cheerleader . . . one of the popular crowd."

He frowned. "Do you have to be a cheerleader to be popular?"

Tara sighed. Poor Uncle Pat. He was so oblivious to what life was like for kids these days.

"No, of course not. But it helps if people know you. And you have to stick around longer than six months to make friends."

He sighed. "Man, I am so sorry," he said.

Tara stopped. "For what, Uncle Pat?"

"For making your life so difficult."

Tara dropped the chamois and hugged his neck. "You didn't make my life difficult. You saved it," she whispered, and then kissed the side of his cheek.

"Well, well," he mumbled, but he was smiling wide as he hugged her back. "I think I'll go out back and get out that iron bench I was talking about. It's a little rusty. I might need to repaint it before it will be decent to sit on."

"It'll look great," Tara said. "I just need to vacuum out the inside of the car and then I'm done."

Her uncle went one way while she went another. A few minutes later she was head down in the front seat of the car with the roar of the vacuum loud in her ears. She shoved the hose underneath the passenger side of the seat and as she did, heard a clink. Something metal had gone into the vacuum. Yikes. She'd better make sure it wasn't something important.

She backed out of the car and then took the bag off the vacuum and carried it to the garbage bin, pulled out an old newspaper, then dumped the contents of the vacuum bag onto it.

At first, she didn't see anything that would have made a

metallic sound, but she kept sifting through the dust bunnies until her fingers connected with something solid. She pulled it out, wiped it off, then frowned.

"Where on earth did this—"

All of a sudden, the world began to spin—spinning her right into Bethany Fanning's head.

Chapter Eight

Bethany hated the closet. He only let her out to go to the bathroom. Now she sat among the litter of fast-food wrappers and empty soda cans. She couldn't stand it anymore. She looked at her hands. They were filthy and she had a splinter under her nail from trying to catch the door as he slammed it shut. All of a sudden she heard footsteps and scooted as far back into the corner as she could get.

The door opened. "Please, let me go. I'm sorry I was mean to you."

Tears filled his eyes and rolled down his cheeks. "You laughed at me. You called me a creep and told me to get lost."

"I know, I know. And I'm sorry. But what I said to you doesn't make it okay to do this to me. I want to go home. I want my Mother."

"My mother says not to let people hurt me. You hurt me. It's too late now."

The door shut.

Once again, Bethany was alone. But this time something was different. It was the first time he'd said that—about it being too late. What did this mean? What was going to happen to her?

Tara gasped, then looked down at the ring she'd taken out of the dust. It was pewter colored metal in the shape of a skull. Just like the skull and barbed wire tattoo on Flynn's arm. Could this be his? It was under the seat where he'd been sitting. But why had it had been a conduit to Bethany? She needed to talk to Flynn to find out. She wiped it off and slipped it into her pocket as she stood up. If this last vision was real, it just confirmed Bethany's time was running out. She wasn't hurt yet, but she might be, soon. She clasped the ring in her fist again and closed her eyes, but nothing happened. Whatever this was, it wasn't strong enough to keep her connected. She had to do something, but she wasn't sure what. She headed for the back yard.

"Hey, Uncle Pat."

He was scrubbing the rust off the iron bench.

"I'm here," he said, as he stopped and waved.

"I need to use the car again, okay?"

He glanced at his watch. It was almost three-thirty. "Are you planning to be home before night?"

"I think so. Why? Did you need the car?"

"No, no. Just making sure I knew your plans."

"I'll call you later."

"Okay, but be please be careful. I don't want to lose you like Bethany's family lost her."

It was the first that Tara knew he'd been worrying. But she knew it wasn't some random pervert on the make all over Stillwater. Whoever had Bethany had a personal grudge against her.

"You won't, I promise," she said, and hurried back toward the car.

It did occur to her as she was driving away that Emmit Broyles was still a threat, but she felt confident that Millicent and Henry would forewarn her enough to stay out of danger. Besides, she couldn't exactly go into hiding until all of this got sorted out. DeeDee was already dead. It was Bethany whose days might be numbered.

She drove back to Flynn's house with the ring in her pocket and one eye on the rearview mirror as she went. She didn't really believe she had anything more to fear from Emmit today, but it wasn't smart to be careless.

A short while later she pulled into the driveway and jumped out on the run. She knocked and waited, but no one answered. Then she knocked again, shouting Flynn's name. Still no answer.

He couldn't go missing now. She needed to find him.

Then she thought of his mother. Mona might know.

She jumped back in the car and headed for Eskimo Joe's. Even though it was late afternoon and long past the lunch crowd, the parking lot of Joe's was full—a testament to the fame and popularity of the place. She finally found a place to park and ran the block and a half back to Joe's, then inside through the souvenir shop where the famous Eskimo Joe's logo was on everything they sold, and finally up to the hostess.

"Hi, is Mona O'Mara still here?"

A young woman with short pink hair glanced over her shoulder, as if looking for her, then frowned as she turned back to Tara. "Yeah, I think."

"Could I speak to her, please? It's sort of an emergency."

"Wait here," the girl said, and headed toward the kitchen.

Within a few moments, Mona appeared. She was smiling before she got close enough to speak.

"Hey, I remember you. You're Pat's niece, aren't you?"

"Yes, ma'am," Tara said.

"What's up? Is Pat all right?" Mona asked.

"Yes, Uncle Pat is fine. I need to talk to Flynn, but he's not home. It's really important or I wouldn't bother you like this."

Mona's smile slipped. "I already know about the fight. He called me. And I want to thank you for taking him home."

Tara nodded. "Sure thing. But he's not home now. Do you know where he might be?"

"Not really. He didn't say . . . Oh. Wait. When he was younger, he used to ride his bike out to Boomer Lake. It's quite a ride out, but it's where he and his Dad used to go fish. When something is bothering him and he won't talk about it, he goes out there."

"How do I get there?" Tara asked.

Mona wrote down the directions, then went back to work after a promise from Tara to let her know if something was wrong.

Tara ran back to her car. It was just after four. She didn't understand the impending doom she kept feeling, but knew better than to ignore it.

Within fifteen minutes she was pulling up to one of the boat docks at Boomer Lake. A huge surge of relief went through her when she saw Flynn sitting on the edge with his feet dangling over the water. She felt his anxiety and confusion. She sensed he wasn't going to welcome her arrival, but this was no longer about them. Tara had been hoping for a connection to Bethany ever since her disappearance and this was the first real break she'd had.

She dashed across the ground toward the dock.

When Flynn heard the sound of footsteps behind him, he turned around. Almost instantly, his expression darkened.

"What are you doing here?" he asked.

Tara pulled the ring out of her pocket.

"Is this yours?"

The tone of his voice shifted. "Yeah. It is. Where did you find it?"

"Beneath the seat of the car."

"You could have given it to me at school on Monday. You didn't have to—"

"That's not why I'm here," Tara said, then sat down on the dock beside him. "I need you to answer some questions for me."

The frown came back. Coupled with his bruises and the Band Aids on his face, he looked miserable.

"Look, Moon girl, this isn't a good time for me."

"Fine, because this isn't about you. It's about Bethany."

"Bethany? I already told you she and—"

"Will you please wait for me to ask stuff before you start talking?"

He shrugged, then looked away.

Tara grabbed his arm. "Look at me, Flynn."

He sighed, then looked back. "What?"

"The ring . . . what is the connection between it and Bethany?"

"She gave it to me."

The expression on Tara's face was one of instant understanding. "Then I was right," she muttered. "I'm connecting through . . . oh, never mind. But why isn't the connection lasting? Why do I keep losing her?"

"What are you talking about?" Flynn asked.

Tara knew the next few minutes were going to be key to whether or not they could make their relationship work, because to get what she needed to help Bethany, she was going to have to tell him the truth about herself.

"I need to tell you something," Tara said. "It's going to sound weird, and you're probably not going to believe me."

"Just spit it out, Tara. My head is hurting too much to try and figure out what you're talking about."

"Sorry." She took his hand, then looked him straight in the eyes. "Here's the deal," she said. "I'm psychic, and I've been getting these flashes about Bethany but couldn't—"

"Whoa, whoa, whoa! Back up a minute, Moon girl. What did you just say?"

Tara sighed. "Psychic . . . as in able to know and see stuff other people can't. I've been like this my whole life. It's no big deal to me."

"But it's a big deal that you want me to believe this."

"I don't care whether or not you believe me. I just care that you're willing to help me so I can figure out where Bethany is."

"Why do you think you can do something the Stillwater police and the state bureau of investigation agents can't do?"

"I don't think it. I *know* it. I just need something stronger to connect to. Do you have anything of Bethany's at your house . . . like a photo she gave you, or a scarf, or—"

""No. What I didn't give back, I threw away."

"You still had the ring."

His face flushed angrily. "Yes, but only because my dad has one just like it. I made the mistake of telling her that when we were dating. She gave it to me for my birthday. I kept it only because it's like my Dad's, not because she gave it to me."

"Okay, okay. I wasn't trying to dig into your business here. I just need something to get me tuned back in to Bethany."

Flynn shook his head. "I'm sorry, Moon girl, but you're too far out for me to—"

Tara was ticked. She hated it when people belittled what she did, and hated that this was the only way they would believe.

"Fine. You want proof? You got a Batman bike for Christmas when you were nine."

He looked startled, then shook his head. "Mom could have told you that."

"But she didn't. Your dad told you in his last letter that he's been diagnosed with cancer."

He nearly fell off the dock. "How do you know that?" he whispered. "I haven't even told Mom."

"How do you think?"

He kept shaking his head no, as if the thought of admitting what she was proving to him was too big to take in. Then he fixed her with a curious stare.

"Okay. If you're for real, then figure this one out. Two years ago, my mom lost a ring that used to belong to her mother. She's been sad about it ever since."

A scene flashed into Tara's head—a place she'd seen before. In Flynn's house. Earlier today. When she'd watched him taking painkillers in the kitchen.

"There's a place on your kitchen counters behind the faucet, where the grouting has broken away. The ring is down in there between the walls. If I prove that to you, will you help me?"

"Yes."

"Get in the car."

"I rode my bike."

"So, put it in the trunk. And hurry."

Within fifteen minutes, they were pulling back into Flynn's driveway. He dumped his bike on the front porch, then led the way inside to the kitchen.

"Let me look," he said, and peered down into the crack. He frowned at her, as if accusing her of a lie. "There's nothing there."

"Get me a flashlight," Tara said.

He pulled one out of a nearby drawer, handed it to her, then watched as she climbed up onto the counter on her hands and knees and leaned forward, aiming the light at an angle into the crack. Almost instantly, she caught a glimmer of metal.

"Fishing pole. Do you have a fishing pole . . . with a hook?"

"Yeah, but—"

"Just get the pole. I keep telling you we're wasting time."

He left the room, but came back shortly with a rod and reel.

Tara let out some line, then frowned. "Hold the flashlight for me. I need to use both hands."

Flynn did as she asked, watching the intent expression on her face as she ran the line down into the crack. It took her a few tries before it caught, but when she began to pull it up, there was a look of satisfaction on her face. Seconds later, she pulled the ring up and out and put it in Flynn's hand with a disgusted sigh.

"Here. Now. This is going to have to do for proof because we can't waste any more of Bethany's time."

Flynn was stunned. He kept looking at the ring, then looking at Tara.

"For real?"

She nodded.

He shook his head as he put the ring in a cup in the cabinet to show his mom later. "What do you need?"

"Something that belongs to Bethany . . . only I can't go to her parents. They wouldn't believe me anyway."

"What about Davis?" Flynn asked.

Tara's eyes widened. Yeah. The current squeeze. Then she frowned. "But you guys just had the fight from hell."

He shrugged. "If you think you can help find her, I don't mind getting pounded again."

"I mind. You're not going to get pounded. But I do need you to come with me. I don't know where he lives, and I need all the backup I can get."

"Dang. I couldn't go and get myself an ordinary girlfriend," Flynn muttered, as he put his arm around Tara and followed her out the door.

Tara stopped. "So, I'm your girlfriend?"

"Far as I'm concerned," he said.

She grinned, then handed him the car keys. "You drive, okay? It'll be quicker since you know the way."

"Whatever," Flynn said, and started the car. A short while later they were on the other side of town and pulling up the drive that led to an imposing two story structure. "Here it is," he said.

"Wow! What does his Dad do for a living?" Tara asked.

"He's in oil. That's all I know."

They parked the car and headed for the front door together. But it was Tara who rang the doorbell. And it was Tara who stepped in front of Flynn when Davis Breedlove answered the door. He didn't look any better than Flynn did, but the expression on his face went from shock to fury as he spotted Flynn.

"What? Did you come back so I could finish kicking your ass?"

Tara grabbed Davis's arm before he could move.

Step back. I've got this.

"Not now, Millicent. I need him in one piece."

"Who the hell is Millicent and what are you muttering about?" Davis asked, as he yanked out of Tara's grasp.

"OMG . . . Davis, do not use the word hell and Millicent in the same sentence and expect me to be responsible for the next five minutes of your life," Tara said.

Davis looked as confused as Flynn felt. "Get off my property," he said, and started to shut the door in their faces. Then all of a sudden, he went flying backwards, sliding across the slick marble floor on the seat of his sweat pants, although no one had even come close to touching him.

Flynn's mouth dropped. "What just happened?"

"Millicent. She doesn't like it when people dis me."

"Millicent?"

"She's one of my peeps," Tara said, with a grin.

Now you're talking.

Tara stepped into the doorway. "Look, Davis. I'm really sorry about that. I told you Millicent wouldn't be happy."

Davis was crawling to his feet, but keeping his distance. He didn't know what had happened, but he didn't want close to her again.

"The reason we're here is I think I have a way to find Bethany. Will you help me?"

All of a sudden, she had his attention. "Like how?" he asked.

"Has Bethany given you anything of hers . . . a photo she signed to you . . . anything that came from her?"

"What is this . . . twenty questions? I thought you said you could find her," he mumbled.

"I told you . . . I think I can find her."

"You're nuts. No wonder Beth and her friends call you lunatic."

Oh no he didn't.

"Ohmygod," Tara said, and watched Davis go flying across the floor on his butt once more. "Look, Davis . . . if you want to stay upright, stop dissin' me, savvy?"

He nodded, but looked like he might start to cry.

"Then get up," Tara said. "I don't have all day."

For the first time since their arrival, his bluff and bluster was gone and he was on the verge of panic. "What's happening? How are you doing that to me?"

Tara sighed. "I'm not doing it. Millicent is doing it."

Flynn held up his hand. "Don't ask," he said. "Just help her."

"What good is it going to do you to look at a picture of Bethany?"

"I don't want to look at it. I need to hold something that was hers so I can connect *to* her."

He frowned. "So you can what?"

"Connect! Connect! I'm psychic, damn it."

Davis stared, and then all of a sudden, he burst into laughter. "You are a lunatic. Certifiable."

That does it!

"Don't, Millicent!" Tara shouted. "I need him in one piece, thank you."

Fine. I won't even touch him.

All of a sudden, a huge commotion sounded in the room behind where Davis was standing.

"What the hell?" he said, and dashed into his father's library.

Books were flying from the shelves. Magazines were levitating while the ink pen on the desk in front of the window went flying past Davis's head, and came to rest in the back of an overstuffed leather chair like an arrow into a target.

He gave Tara a look of panic, and then ducked as a pair of books hit the floor behind him.

"Make it stop," he begged.

"Millicent. Please," Tara begged.

I'll be in the car.

"Thank you," she muttered, then turned to Davis. "Get up. Go get me something that Bethany gave you and hurry."

He didn't hesitate, but ran from the library, leaving them in the middle of the chaos.

Flynn was in a state of shock, but wisely kept his thoughts to himself.

"Uh . . . Moon girl . . . "

She held up her hand. "Just hang with me here."

He nodded, then sat as Davis came running back into the room.

"Will this do? Bethany gave it to me after we started going steady." He gave Flynn a nervous glance.

It was a photo of her in a silver frame, and she'd even signed it, Love, Bethany.

"This should do it," Tara said, and held out her hand.

Within seconds, she shot straight into Bethany's head— seeing everything Bethany was seeing—feeling everything Bethany was feeling, including the fear and a growing sense of hopelessness.

She didn't know that Flynn caught her as she staggered. Or that she was looking straight at Davis without seeing him. From the moment she'd touched the frame, she gone.

Bethany was staring at the closet door with her heart in her throat. He'd been pacing on the little porch outside for what seemed like an hour. She didn't know what was going to happen, but sensed it wasn't going to be good. Ever since he'd arrived this morning, he'd been different, as if he'd come to some kind of decision.

Then the pacing stopped. She held her breath, her gaze fixed to the door. The knob started turning and Bethany shuddered. Is this it? Is this the day I die?

He walked in. He'd been crying again. Did this mean he'd had a change of heart? Was he finally going to let her go?

"Charlie . . . I want you to know I'll never tell."

Then she saw him shudder.

"Dead women tell no tales," he said.

Her heart stopped. Had she read him wrong?

"What do you mean?" He came towards her with his hands out and pulled her out of the closet.

"I'm sorry," he said. "It's all your fault this has to happen."

"Noooo!" Bethany screamed, and then his hands were at her throat.

"Noooo!!! He killed her!"

Tara threw the frame on the sofa

Flynn grabbed her and held her. He'd seen enough already to believe her—enough to be afraid she was right.

Davis was in shock.

"What happened? What just happened?" he cried.

Tara shoved out of Flynn's arms and swiped angrily at her face. "Why?" she cried to the forces that gave her the visions. "Why wait until now when it's too late?"

Flynn grabbed her arm. "Talk to us, Tara. We're in the dark, here."

"I saw someone named Charlie grab her by the throat. Just now. Just now."

Davis sank into a nearby chair. Flynn's eyes went wide with shock, but Tara was in fighting mode.

"Who's Charlie? Who do you know named Charlie?"

Davis and Flynn looked at each other, then Davis answered first. "I know a couple of guys. Charlie Samson and

Charles Friend."

"And there's Charlie Pratt and John Charles Washington," Flynn added.

Tara shoved her hands through her hair and then turned in a little circle, so upset and so frustrated she couldn't think. All of a sudden, Henry was standing by the French doors leading out to a verandah.

"What?" Tara asked, and then noticed Henry was pointing down at the floor.

She raced over. The floor was littered with books that Millicent had tossed from the shelves. She kept looking, but didn't understand, and then she saw it. A yearbook from Stillwater High.

"Henry! You're are so smart!" She grabbed the yearbook and headed back to Davis and Flynn. "Here," she said, and thrust the book at Flynn. "Show me! Show me the guys named Charlie in here."

"This is last year's yearbook," Davis said. "Look in sophomores and juniors."

"Right," Flynn said, and began leafing through it quickly. He found the first two quickly.

"Here's John Charles . . . and this is Charles Samson. They're juniors this year."

Tara looked. Neither of them were the guy she'd seen choking Bethany.

"No. Neither one of them," she said. "Find the others."

Flynn flipped to the juniors. "This is Charles Friend. He's a senior this year with us. Charlie Pratt was a senior in this book, so he graduated, but he was in Special Ed. I don't even know if he's still in Stillwater."

"It's not Charles Friend," Tara said. "What if it's someone who didn't even go to school here?"

Flynn shuffled through a couple more pages until he got to the senior class, then quickly found the last Charles. "Here he is. This is Charlie Pratt. Like I said, there was something wrong with his mind. He couldn't learn stuff like the rest of us, but I don't think he would—"

Tara gasped. "That's him," she said. "This is the guy who kidnapped her. Do you know where he lives?"

"I don't," Flynn said, and looked at Davis.

"I don't either," Davis said.

Tara looked back at the photo of Bethany. The sadness was overwhelming. Without thinking, she picked the frame back up and to her shock, was once again, back with Bethany.

She was flattened against the closet wall, holding up her hands like claws and. Charlie was sitting in the doorway with long scratch marks on his cheeks, sobbing uncontrollably.

"I'm sorry, I'm sorry," he kept saying. "I don't think I can do this."

Charlie pushed himself up from the floor and with one last look back at Bethany, locked the closet door, once again shutting her inside, then staggered from the room.

Tara squealed. "He couldn't do it!" she cried. "Bethany isn't dead. I lost connection for a minute, that's all. We've got to find out where he's holding her. He might change his mind."

"I'm so confused," Davis said. "How do you do this?"

"I don't know, I just do. Who do you know who can find Charlie Pratt's home? Even if that's not where he took her, it's a good place to start looking."

Flynn grabbed the yearbook and began leafing through the senior pictures all over again.

"Who was that guy he used to hang out with? He drove that old VW bus, remember?"

Davis leaned over Flynn's shoulder as they both scanned the photos. Suddenly, Davis's finger stabbed at a photo.

"There! That's the guy. Taylor French."

"Yeah," Flynn said. "Way to go, man."

Davis beamed, and then looked a little embarrassed that he was connecting so personally with someone who was supposed to be the enemy.

"We don't have time for this," Tara said. "How can we find Taylor French?"

Flynn grinned. "He busses tables at Joe's."

"No way," Tara said.

Flynn nodded.

"Call your mom and ask her if he's at work," she cried.

Flynn grabbed his cell and walked a short distance away to make the call as Tara and Davis stared at each other.

"I'm sorry about the mess," Tara said, pointing to the books and the ruined back of the leather chair. No telling what that had cost.

"Yeah ... well ... I don't really get how it happened. I don't even know what I saw."

"Welcome to my world," Tara muttered, then Flynn was back.

"He was there. Get in the car. I know where Charlie lives."

Tara headed for the door with Flynn right behind her. She was on the threshold when she realized Davis wasn't with them.

"Hey!" she yelled. "Are you coming or what?"

He didn't have to be asked twice. He was out the door and in the back seat of Tara's car before she got her seat belt buckled. Seconds later, they were off.

Chapter Nine

Charlie Pratt's home was in a trailer park on the east side of Stillwater. As Tara, Flynn and Davis pulled into the trailer park and then turned down the first street, Tara began to scan the lot numbers.

"Look for number fifteen," Flynn said.

Tara began counting down the numbers as they drove.

"There!" Davis shouted. "Next to the last on the left."

Flynn wheeled up to the trailer and put the car in park. It was an old blue and white trailer with part of the skirting missing and a broken birdbath next to the steps. Someone had thrown a couple of old tires onto the roof in an obvious attempt to hold down loose roofing strips. All in all, it was a pretty sad sight.

"Now what?" Flynn asked.

"Both of you come with me," Tara said. "I may get kicked out and I don't want to dodge fists in the process."

Flynn frowned. "Look, if this is dangerous—"

Tara grabbed him by the arm. "Flynn! Bethany is the one who's in danger. So come on."

She got out of the car and started up the steps with Flynn and Davis flanking her. She took a deep breath, and then knocked forcefully several times.

Seconds later, she began hearing the frantic yapping of a small dog, and then a man cursing. The door swung inward. The woman standing there looked tired and beaten down by more than her husband's fists. The years had not been kind to her.

"Yeah? What do you want?" she asked.

"Shirley . . . tell 'em we ain't buyin' nothin'!" the man

yelled.

"We aren't selling anything," Tara said quickly. "We're trying to find Charlie."

Shock spread across her face. "Charlie? What do y'all want with my boy?"

"He isn't here?" Tara asked.

"No," she said, and started to close the door. "Y'all go on now. Wayne don't like visitors much."

Tara put her foot in the crack of the door. "Charlie is in trouble," Tara said. "And we need to find him before he does something he can't take back."

"Whaaat?" Shirley cried.

Wayne yelled from inside. "Y'all get on out of here now a'fore I call the cops."

"Go ahead and call them," Tara yelled back. "Because when they find your son, he's going to be under arrest."

Shirley Pratt gasped. "What are you talking about?" she cried. "What kind of trouble is Charlie in?"

By now, Wayne Pratt was out of his chair and lumbering toward the door. Tara felt his fury and it was all she could do to stand her ground. The door swung inward as Wayne roughly shoved his wife out of the way.

He was massive—at least five inches over six feet tall and weighing a good three hundred and fifty pounds or more. His clothes were stained and dirty and there was a good six inches of his belly showing from beneath the shirt. He was reaching toward Tara when Flynn suddenly stepped between them.

"I wouldn't," Flynn said softly.

"Tell me where Charlie is before it's too late," Tara repeated.

"Too late for what?" Wayne growled.

"He's already going to be charged with kidnaping and assault, but he hasn't killed her yet."

For the first time Tara had their full attention. "What in hell are you talking about?" he asked.

"Bethany Fanning. Charlie is the one who took Bethany Fanning."

Tara heard his mother cry out, and then saw her run toward the door. Shirley shoved her husband aside, and then clutched at Tara.

"How do you know this? How do you know?"

"I just do," Tara said. "Now think! If you want your son to stay alive, you need to help me find him. If he kills Bethany, he'll get the death sentence and you know it."

"Oh dear God," his mother cried. "I don't know where he is. I have no idea. He's been gone a lot lately."

Tara's heart dropped. "Look. If you could just bring me something of his, I might figure it out on my own."

"Bring you somethin? What do you mean, bring you somethin'? Is this just some con to get our stuff?" Wayne grumbled.

"No!" Tara screamed, and then focused her attention on the mother. "Go into Charlie's room. Bring me something that's his. I don't want to keep it. I just need to hold it."

"It's a con! You get back in here and leave them be!" Wayne said.

But Charlie's mother knew better. "No, Wayne, I told you two days ago something was wrong with Charlie. I heard him crying at night when he thought we were all asleep. Charlie is almost twenty. He don't cry like he used to anymore. Something's wrong."

She pushed past her husband and ran. Seconds later she was back with a handful of CDs.

"Will these do? He plays them all the time."

Tara took them out of her hands, and the moment she did, felt faint. She didn't know Flynn grabbed her to keep from falling again, or that he and Davis traded panicked looks. She was locked into Charlie Watt's despair. She could see water . . . and a cabin . . . and a whole lot of trees—and an old yellow truck.

"Does your family have a lake house?" Tara asked.

Wayne Pratt laughed. "Do we look like we got us a fancy lake house? Hell no, we ain't got no lake house."

But Shirley knew better. "My father . . . Charlie's

grandpa . . . had an old fishing cabin out at the lake. He used to take Charlie out there all the time when he was little. It belongs to my step-mom, but she's in Denver. Been there for a couple of months now."

Tara kept seeing an old yellow truck with the tag missing parked in front of it.

"Does he drive a yellow truck, and are there a pair of pine trees in front of the house and a big oak at the back?"

"Yes . . . yes. How do you know that?"

"And the number on the lot . . . is it 104?"

"Oh lord, oh lord . . . yes it is," she wailed.

Tara felt a sense of relief at knowing she was tuned in to the right place. "How do we get there?"

Davis and Flynn looked at each other, stunned by what they were witnessing. How could it be this easy? The police had been looking for Bethany for over a week and Tara just touches stuff and knows? This was way past wacked.

When the woman began giving directions, Tara knew she was going to get confused.

"Flynn! Are you paying attention to this? I will get lost if I'm driving."

"I'm listening, Moon girl. You stay connected to Charlie. I've got your back on the rest."

Charlie's mother was weeping as she finished. "Are you sure about this?" she asked.

Tara clutched the CDs against her belly and closed her eyes and saw him walking back into the cabin carrying a rifle.

"Oh no," Tara gasped, then opened her eyes and grabbed Shirley Pratt's arm. "Mrs. Pratt, does your family own a gun?"

"Yes."

"Would you please look and see if it's still here?"

"Ain't no one looking for my gun!" Wayne yelled.

"Please!" Tara begged.

Charlie's mother hesitated only briefly, then once more pushed past her husband and left.

There was a long uncomfortable silence as Wayne glared at the trio on his stoop. Then suddenly, there was a long, mournful wail.

"Uh oh," Tara said, and looked at Davis and Flynn. "I'm betting the gun is AWOL."

Shirley Pratt came running back, her hands clutched at her heart as if holding it would keep her in one piece.

"It's gone. Sure as God, it's gone!" she cried.

Tara turned to Davis and Flynn. "We've got to get out there, and fast." Then she gave Shirley Pratt one last task. "Mrs. Pratt, I need you to call the police. Tell them what you just told us about how to get to that cabin. Tell them to hurry and pray that we get there before Charlie uses that gun."

"Me? Call the cops on my own son?"

"How do you think Stillwater is going to view you two when they find out it was your son who kidnaped Bethany . . . that you knew it and did nothing?" Flynn asked.

"Oh lord, oh lord," she moaned, and covered her face.

"We ain't callin' no cops," Wayne growled.

Shirley turned on him angrily. "Yes, I am," she shrieked. "And you're not gonna stop me! If Charlie has turned into this kind of person, he has you to thank for it."

"We'll be calling them, too," Tara said. "But like Flynn said, it will help coming from you, too."

Shirley nodded. "Go on and do what you gotta do," she said. "I'll call the cops."

Tara headed for the car. Flynn and Davis were, once again, right behind her. Flynn slid into the driver's seat, then winced at the pain rippling around his belly as he buckled the seat belt around him.

Davis wasn't any better. He groaned aloud as he folded himself into the confines of the back seat. The longer time passed since their fight this morning, the stiffer they were getting.

"If you guys think you're sore, think of how Bethany feels. She's been locked in a closet for more than a week and scared out of her mind."

"Son-of-a-bitch!" Davis muttered.

A muscle jerked in Flynn's jaw, but he put his anger into

focus and headed for Lake Carl Blackwell as fast as the law would allow.

"Davis. Call the police," Tara said.

Davis began making the call.

"Flynn, do you have your ring with you?"

He nodded.

"I need it."

"Oh. Sure. It's in the pocket of my jeans . . . right side," he added.

Tara's eyes widened. Without giving herself time to think about what she was doing, she thrust her fingers into the gap of his pocket and dug downward.

"Hey, Moon girl, you're tickling," Flynn said.

"Do not look at me," she muttered, as she finally got to the bottom of the pocket and felt the ring. "Thank God," she muttered, and pulled it out.

Way to go, Missy.

"Can it, Millicent. I have enough trouble as it is. If you want to be helpful, go find out what's happening with Charlie Pratt."

Send Henry. I'm riding in the back seat with the chunk.

Tara snorted. "It's not chunk, it's *hunk*. You are so wacked. Now beat it. I've got a long-distance call to make here, and the reception isn't all it could be."

Flynn pretended he didn't notice that Tara was talking to herself.

"You're going to call Bethany?" Davis asked.

"In a manner of speaking," Tara said, and then cupped the ring in both hands and took a deep breath.

Within seconds, she was sick to her stomach with fear.

"Hurry, Flynn," she said softly, her blind gaze fixed on a scene that only she could see.

Flynn muttered beneath his breath as he pressed even harder on the accelerator while Davis, in the back seat, was talking to the cops.

All of a sudden the closet door was open. Bethany looked up and then screamed. *"Charlie, what are you going to do with that gun?"*

Charlie was shaking, but he kept the gun pointed straight at her.

"Daddy says when I do something bad he will whip me. I don't want Daddy to whip me anymore. It hurts. I hurts real bad."

Bethany's mind was racing, trying to think of what to say that would stop this madness.

"You didn't do anything bad, Charlie. That was me. I'm the one who laughed, remember? You were just trying to help. Right?

Charlie blinked. "I was gonna help you start your car."

"Right! But I was rude, wasn't I?"

Charlie nodded.

"So if I say I'm sorry, and I explain to everyone that it was my fault, then we can all go home and this will be over. Can we do that, Charlie? I will tell them it was my fault."

Charlie hesitated, then raised the rifle. "No one ever listens to me. They say I'm stupid, but I'm not. I'm just slow. You shouldn't have laughed."

Tara's head flew back against the seat as her eyes popped open. She looked around wildly, then grabbed hold of the dash.

"Flynn! How far are we from the cabin?"

"A couple of minutes, I think."

She grabbed his arm. "Hurry! Charlie is going to shoot her."

"Are you serious?" Davis cried. "How do you know this stuff?"

Tara rolled her eyes. "You are one dense puppy. We've already been down this road," she muttered. Then she changed the subject. "Did you call the police?"

"Yeah, but I'm not sure they—"

"Hit re-dial and give me the phone!" Tara cried.

Davis frowned, but did what she asked. Tara grabbed it, then waited for the call to be answered.

"911, what is your emergency?" the dispatcher said.

"I need to talk to either Detective Rutherford or Detective Allen. It has to do with Bethany Fanning, the girl who disappeared."

"One moment while I patch you through," the dispatcher said.

"Hurry!" Tara begged.

It seemed like forever before someone answered. When they did, Tara could hear sirens in the background.

"Detective Rutherford."

"Detective Rutherford, this is Tara Luna . . . from high school. You talked to me, remember? I don't have time to explain, but Davis Breedlove, Flynn O'Mara and I know where Bethany Fanning is."

"We're already responding to a phone call from Breedlove and I'm warning you, young lady, it's a crime to make false statements to the police."

"The statements aren't false and the reason I'm calling is to tell you is to hurry. Charlie Pratt has his father's rifle. He's planning to kill Bethany and dump her body in Boomer Lake."

"Listen, you!" the detective cried. "How do you know all—"

"Just hurry! I think we're here. Gotta go!"

"Wait! Wait! Don't go—"

Tara tossed the cell into the back seat as Flynn hit the brakes beside an old yellow truck with a missing license tag.

"Oh man . . . there's Charlie's old car. Tara . . . Moon girl . . . you were right."

"Duh," Tara said, and then grabbed the door handle. "Hurry. He's gonna shoot her."

"What if he shoots us?" Davis cried.

Run, Tara, run.

"Run!" Tara screamed.

After all they'd witnessed today, Flynn and Davis didn't have to be told twice. They flew past her, leaped the steps and kicked in the door. Tara was far enough behind them that she didn't see who shot who, but she heard a scream, then a single gun shot. Her heart was in her throat as she leaped the steps. She caught a flash of yellow from the corner of her eye as she dashed into the one-room cabin, and then all her focus centered on Flynn and Davis, who had Charlie Pratt pinned beneath them in the middle of the floor. Charlie was fighting and crying, but they had him outnumbered.

"Tara. Get Bethany!" Flynn yelled.

Tara spun. The flash of yellow she'd seen had been Bethany, huddled in the closet.

Tara dashed toward the closet.

Bethany crawled to her knees then grabbed onto Tara's outstretched hands. "You found me. Thank God that you found me. I want to go home. Please take me home."

Tara touched Bethany's face gently. "Hang in there honey. You'll be home soon. In no time."

Then she ran back into the kitchen, saw a length of rope on the floor beside the door and took it to boys who still had Charlie pinned. They tied him up and then Flynn sat on top of him as Davis ran to the closet and helped Bethany to her feet.

She stumbled.

Tara was on one side of Bethany and Davis was on the other as they exited the front door.

"Sit here," she said, helping Bethany down onto the steps. Davis ran back inside with Flynn. Moments later Tara began hearing sirens. "Flynn! Davis! The police are here!"

"We're coming out!" Flynn said.

Charlie Pratt emerged from the cabin with his hands tied behind his back. His nose was bleeding and there was a cut just above one eyebrow. Tara eyed him cautiously. He didn't look so scary now. In fact, Charlie was the one who looked scared.

"Move," Davis said, and pushed Charlie forward just as a parade of police cruisers suddenly appeared over the small hill, followed by an ambulance.

The heat is here.

Tara grinned. *Millicent must be stoked. She's sending me messages in cop speak.*

Davis had tears on his face as he picked Bethany up in his arms.

"You're alive, Bets, and that's all that matters. You're gonna be all right," he said.

"Oh, Davis. I thought I was going to die," Bethany cried.

"I'm going with her to the hospital," Davis said.

Bethany hid her face on Davis's shoulder as he carried her toward the arriving ambulance.

Suddenly, police were everywhere, spilling out of cruisers and coming at them from every direction.

Tara saw the detectives, Rutherford and Allen, rushing forward as Flynn gladly handed Charlie over to a half-dozen uniformed officers.

Rutherford's face was flushed as he reached Tara and Flynn.

"That's the guy who had Bethany," Tara said. "His name is Charlie Pratt. Flynn and Davis stopped him only seconds before he shot her."

"The rifle is still in the cabin where we took him down," Flynn said. "We didn't mess with it."

"Damn it, you kids should have waited for the authorities. You could have been killed," Detective Allen said.

Tara frowned. "If we'd waited, Bethany would be dead. There wasn't any time to wait. Did you call her parents? She keeps asking for her mother."

Rutherford sighed. "We will . . . now that we know what to tell them."

But it was Allen who asked the question Tara had been dreading.

"How in hell did you kids figure this out? How did you find her?"

Flynn looked at Tara, then shrugged. "I'm at a loss for words," he said.

Tara sighed. "Would you believe a little bird told us?"

"No," both men said in unison.

"I didn't think so," Tara muttered.

"See that bench over there? Boy, you wait for Detective Allen over there. Miss Luna, you wait for me in my cruiser. We'll be needing your statements before you can leave," Rutherford said.

Tara glanced toward the west and the swiftly setting sun. "I need to call Uncle Pat so he doesn't worry about where I am."

"Yeah, and I need to call Mom," Flynn added. "I don't want her getting a second-hand version of this."

"Make it quick," Rutherford said.

Tara and Flynn nodded, then looked at each other. Flynn just kept shaking his head.

"You're something else, Moon girl. You saved Bethany's life. You know that, don't you?"

Tara shrugged. "You and Davis helped." Then she glanced at the detective. "We'd better hurry," she said. "I don't think the police are too happy with us."

"Yeah, but Bethany sure is."

Tara grinned. "Yeah," she said, then they quickly parted company to make their calls.

Flynn walked a short distance away as he dialed his mom's number, while Tara quickly dialed her uncle's cell phone. It rang four times before he picked up.

"Hello?"

"Uncle Pat, it's me, Tara."

"Hi honey. Are you on your way home?"

"No. That's why I'm calling. I'm going to be a little bit late."

"Why? Are you having car trouble?"

"No. Nothing like that, Uncle Pat. Here's the thing . . . by accident, Flynn, Davis Breedlove, and I stumbled onto where that missing girl, Bethany Fanning was being held. Long story short, we sort of rescued her right before the guy was about to kill her."

"Oh dear lord! Tara! Are you all right? Where are you? I'll catch a cab."

"We're okay, Uncle Pat. Flynn and I figured the news would spread pretty fast, and we didn't want you or his Mom to hear something second-hand. The police want to talk to us, so we can't leave until they've taken our statements and stuff."

"I want to know where you are. I'm coming out."

"It's out at Boomer Lake, Uncle Pat. I don't know how to tell you where we are because after we figured out where she was, Flynn drove here. Wait and I'll let him tell you. He's talking to his mom, right now."

"He's talking to Mona? Then never mind. I'll give her a call and we'll both be out."

"You have her phone number?" Tara asked in surprise.

"Never mind about that," he said. "You two are the ones who have some explaining to do. Now what's the address?"

Tara told him the lot number and the name of the road.

"But, Uncle Pat, there's really no need to come out. As soon as the police are through talking to us, we'll be coming home," Tara said.

"I said, we'll be out there," he repeated.

Tara sighed. She had a feeling this wasn't going to be good. To explain what had happened, she was going to have to bring up the psychic stuff to Uncle Pat again, and he wasn't going to be happy.

"Okay," she said. "See you."

He disconnected.

She glanced at Flynn. He had just finished talking to his mom, too. Tara walked over.

"Was she upset?"

"In a word, yes," he said.

"Are you in trouble?"

"It's hard to say," he said. "She kept crying. How about you?"

Tara rolled her eyes. "You're not gonna like this, but Uncle Pat is calling your mom. He said they're both coming out here."

Flynn's eyes widened. "Calling Mom? He knows her number?"

Tara sighed. "Looks like it."

Flynn frowned. "What do you think about that?"

"I'm trying not to think about it," Tara muttered, then pointed at Detective Rutherford. "Looks like he's out of patience."

"What are you gonna tell him?" Flynn asked.

"The truth."

"I'm not sure what that is," Flynn said. "I saw it, but I'm still not sure I know what I saw."

"Over here," Detective Rutherford called, pointing at Tara while Detective Allen took Flynn by the arm and led him aside.

Tara's steps were dragging as she headed for the cop. How was she going to explain this?

I've got your back.

"Don't, Millicent!" Tara whispered quickly. "I just have to tell them what happened. We're not in trouble and no one's mad at me. Don't give them a reason to be . . . please."

Tara didn't get an answer, which made her nervous, but her life being as lunatic as it was, she could only hope Millicent managed to maintain.

"All right, Miss Luna. Have a seat."

"I'm good," Tara said, and leaned against his cruiser.

"Fine," Rutherford said, then fixed her with a steady look. "Talk. How did you find out who had Bethany Fanning and where she was being held?"

Chapter Ten

Rutherford wasn't happy with Tara, and she didn't have to be a psychic ghost-talker to know it. She didn't know if it was because three teenagers had found Bethany when the police and the state OSBI had not, or that he thought she was somehow involved in her being taken. Either way, it didn't bode well for her. Still, she wasn't worried. If the detective didn't believe what Flynn and Tara told him, once Bethany calmed down, she'd be able to corroborate their statements.

"So, Miss Luna, we meet again," Rutherford began.

Tara didn't see a need to answer the obvious, and merely nodded.

Hang tough. Don't let them crack you.

It's break, Millicent . . . break. Don't let them break you, and I'm not in trouble so don't go causing me any. Please.

Whatever.

"I'm not sure where to begin," Rutherford said. "So why don't you tell me how you came to know where Bethany Fanning was."

Tara sighed. Lord. Why did everything have to be so difficult? "I can tell you," Tara said. "But you're not going to like it."

Rutherford frowned. "Try me."

"Sometimes I just know stuff . . . okay? I get pictures in my head. I go from there."

Rutherford's jaw went slack. Tara could almost see the gears grinding in his brain, sifting through facts he knew to a premise he did not.

"What are you trying to say here?" he asked.

"I'm psychic."

"Crap on a stick!" Rutherford muttered, then had the

grace to look embarrassed. "I'm sorry. That was entirely inappropriate, and I apologize."

"It's okay," Tara said. "I've heard worse."

"Come on, Miss Luna. You don't expect me to believe this?"

Tara sighed again. How many times had she heard that phrase in her life?

"I don't expect it, but just once in a while it would be nice," she muttered.

Rutherford was getting angry. She could tell by the vein that was beginning to bulge at the right side of his temple.

"I don't have time to play games. Explain yourself," he ordered.

Tara folded her hands in front of her, like a kid about to recite something they'd memorized for class, then looked him straight in the eye.

"Earlier this year, Bethany Fanning was dating Flynn O'Mara. She gave him a ring. After they broke up, he kept it. This morning I took Flynn home from a car wash we were having to raise money to donate toward the reward Bethany's parents had put up. Later, I found the ring under the seat of my car, and when I picked it up . . . it was like . . . " She frowned. "I'm not sure how to explain it. Sometimes holding something that a person is connected to is like a homing signal for me. It locks me into where they are . . . or what's happening to them. Understand?"

"No."

Tara shrugged, but kept on talking. "Anyway . . . to make a really long story short, it was finding that ring that started everything happening. Then it became a race to find her before Charlie killed her."

"And you know this because . . . "

"Because I saw it," Tara said.

"Because you "saw" Bethany here? At this cabin? With Charlie Pratt? All from holding this ring?"

"Only partly. The rest came after we got Davis involved. He and Bethany are dating now, you see, so the connection to her was much stronger through him. That's when I saw the face of the guy had Bethany."

"You knew Charlie Pratt?"

"No sir. He graduated last year, I was told, and Uncle Pat and I didn't move here until about a month ago."

"So how did you—"

"Um . . . Flynn and I were at Davis's house, and I was holding a framed picture that Bethany had given to Davis. So while I'm holding it, it's like looking at a video . . . and in the video, Bethany calls the guy Charlie and then he turned around and I saw his face. I can't explain why, but I knew he'd been in school with her. Flynn and I were at Davis's house when this happened and we looked in Davis's yearbook at all the guys named Charlie and I found him. Flynn knew where he lived, so we went to his house."

"You went to the Pratt residence?"

"Yes sir. Didn't you get a phone call from Mrs. Pratt, telling you about this?"

"Not to my knowledge."

Suddenly, Wayne Pratt's face slid through Tara's mind, coupled with a towel smeared with blood.

" . . . You have to send a police car to the residence! Mr. Pratt . . . Wayne . . . was mad when we left. He beats his wife. He beat Charlie, too."

"And you know this because you're 'seeing' it?"

Tara frowned. "Sort of. I just saw Wayne's face in my mind and a bloody towel. The rest is just common sense."

Rutherford rolled his eyes and yelled at his partner. "Allen!"

Detective Allen looked up. "Yeah?"

"Bring that kid over here now!"

Flynn and the detective approached quickly. Flynn looked at Tara. She rolled her eyes.

Rutherford pointed at Flynn. "I want to know what his story is."

Allen grimaced. "I'm not sure you do."

"Let me guess . . . it has something to do with Miss Luna

here being psychic."

Detective Allen nodded. "Yeah, actually it does."

"Well, that's just freakin' great," he muttered.

Tara was angry, too. "You'd think we were the ones who committed the crime, instead of rescued the victim," she said. "You don't like my story. Go talk to Bethany. Talk to Davis. His Daddy is rich, which in your book must mean whatever comes out of his mouth is the truth." She took a deep breath. "But in the meantime, I suggest you send someone out to check on Shirley Pratt."

Flynn frowned. "Why, Tara?"

"Because Mrs. Pratt never called the police, that's why."

Flynn's frown turned to worry. "Oh man . . . that can't be good." He turned to Detective Allen. "Please. You gotta believe what Tara says. When we left their house, Mrs. Pratt believed everything Tara had told her. She said Charlie had been crying at night and acting strange. Then when Tara asked her to check and see if their gun was in the house, she started to cry. When she found out it was gone, she freaked out. She promised to call the cops because she knew Charlie was in trouble and was going to be arrested, but she didn't want him to commit murder. It was Charlie's dad who was mad at us the whole time. He might have hurt Mrs. Pratt."

Rutherford sighed, then turned to his partner. "Call it in. Have dispatch send a unit out to the residence. The kid here will give you the address . . . right?"

Flynn nodded.

Tara felt sick, and then Millicent made it worse.

It's not good.

Tara gasped. "Are you serious?"

Everyone turned to look at her, but she was too locked into her conversation with Millicent to notice.

It's not your fault.

Tara started to cry.

It's not your fault.

Flynn grabbed Tara's arm. "Moon girl . . . what's happening? What's wrong?"

"Millicent just told me . . . Mrs. Pratt is really hurt… hurt bad hurt. "

Rutherford grabbed her by the arm. "Who's Millicent? What the hell do you mean?"

Tears were streaming down Tara's face. "She's part of my lunatic life. She's a ghost and she's also one of my best friends."

You know it, chirp.

Rutherford took a step back and began to look around in panic.

"You're talking to ghosts? Here? Now?"

To prove the point, Millicent yanked the notebook out of Rutherford's hand and flung it across the yard.

"Millicent. Stop it!" Tara said. "It doesn't matter what he thinks. They'll know soon enough."

Rutherford looked like he was going to faint, but Allen didn't hesitate. He just headed for their car to use the radio.

"Come here, Moon girl," Flynn said softly, and pulled Tara into his arms.

Tara buried her face against his shoulder and started to sob. She was crying for Bethany, who'd endured a week long nightmare, and she was crying because, in their efforts to find Bethany, they'd gotten Mrs. Pratt hurt, too.

"It's okay, honey," Flynn said softly. "You didn't do anything wrong."

"Mrs. Pratt is hurt because of me," Tara sobbed.

"But, Bethany is alive because of you," he countered. "And you didn't hurt Mrs. Pratt. Her husband did. I know what that kind of life is like. I've seen it time and again. People who stay in those kinds of marriages are just a fight away from dying every day. You didn't do it. You didn't even start it. Charlie did, by kidnaping Bethany in the first place, okay?"

"Here kid," Detective Allen said, as he walked up and handed Tara a handful of tissues. "Don't cry, and your guy here is right."

"Did you send someone to check on her?" Tara asked.

He nodded.

"Was she—"

He sighed, then nodded again. "Pretty bad. She's on the way to the hospital."

"Hey," Flynn said, pointing toward the road. "Here comes my mom . . . and your Uncle Pat."

Tara turned to look. Police were trying to keep them back.

"Let them pass!" Rutherford shouted.

Moments later, Mona O'Mara pulled up in the yard. Tara took one look at her Uncle Pat and then started toward him, the closer she got, the faster she moved, and the more she cried.

He caught her in mid-step, wrapped her in his arms and just held her.

"It's okay, honey. It's okay. I've got you now."

"Oh, Uncle Pat . . . she's hurt. Badly."

His heart nearly stopped. "Bethany Fanning?"

Flynn had his arm around his mother. "No, sir. Charlie Pratt's mother. She helped us figure out where Charlie was holding Bethany, and her husband beat her because of it."

"Dear Lord, I don't understand how you two got mixed up in this," Uncle Pat said, and then hugged Tara even tighter. "But that woman's injury is not your fault."

Flynn nodded in agreement. "You're right. It's not Tara's fault. What she can do is a gift. And that gift saved Bethany's life."

Uncle Pat went still. "Gift? What do you mean?"

Flynn was stunned. He looked at Tara. "He knows . . . right?"

She shrugged. "Yes and no."

"What is everyone talking about?" Mona asked.

Tara took a slow breath, and then looked her Uncle square in the eyes. "We're talking about the fact that I'm psychic . . . that I can not only see, but talk to ghosts. That I've been able to do that my whole life and Uncle Pat doesn't want to believe it."

Flynn shook his head. "After what I witnessed today, I question nothing she says."

"You aren't serious?" Mona asked.

"As a heart attack, Mom. I didn't believe her at first either, but to prove it to me, she found Grandma's ring that you lost. I put it in a cup in the cupboard."

Mona's eyes lit up. "Mama's ring? Are you serious? Where was it?"

"In a crack in the wall behind the kitchen faucet. And before you get all bent out of shape and say there are no such people who are psychics, keep in mind that Tara Luna is my girl and I don't want to hear anybody dissin' her."

Tara held her breath, waiting for her Uncle Pat's reaction to the facts that she was not only psychic, but a psychic who had a boyfriend. She could see confusion and frustration in his face, but there was also an acceptance she hadn't expected.

He cupped his niece's face, and then gently kissed her forehead.

"Like I always said . . . you're just like your mother."

Tara frowned. What did that have to do with—she gasped. "Uncle Pat! Are you saying my Mother could . . . that she saw . . ."

Uncle Pat sighed, then nodded. "Your mother could, and our Mom and our grandmother. Can't say beyond that, but those we knew for sure."

"But why wouldn't you ever talk about it with me?" Tara cried.

Uncle Pat sighed. "I guess I was hoping if I ignored it, it wouldn't happen to you."

"OMG," Tara cried, and then threw her arms around his neck and hugged him. "At last . . . something about me that finally makes sense. I'm not so different, after all."

Uncle Pat frowned. "Why, I had no idea you felt like this."

Mona patted him on the arm, then smiled at Tara. "Men don't mean to, but they're usually oblivious."

Flynn frowned. "Dang, Mom."

Mona patted him, too. "It's all right, honey. We love you anyway."

Tara managed a smile, but took comfort in knowing her

Uncle Pat was okay with everything that had gone down. All her life he'd been the one she'd depended on, but today, she'd found another man who'd been dependable, too.

Flynn.

"Thanks, Flynn," she said softly.

He smiled, and then held out his hand.

Tara looked up at her Uncle. She saw him hesitate, then nod. Tara slipped her hand in Flynn's and they walked a short distance away toward the lake shore.

Behind them, both detectives were talking to the adults, while the crime scene investigation team was gathering evidence from inside the cabin, as well as Charlie's old yellow truck.

Somewhere on the far side of Stillwater, Charlie Pratt's world as he'd known it was coming to an end. He would be in a jail cell next to his father before the night was over, and both would still be behind bars when Shirley Pratt got out of the hospital

It was all about choices, and he and his father had made the wrong ones.

Flynn put his arm around Tara's shoulders as they stared out across the water.

"Hey, Moon girl."

"Yeah?" Tara asked.

"I'm really proud of you."

She sighed. "You are?"

"Yeah."

Tara leaned against him. "Thanks. That means a lot."

There was another long stretch of silence as they watched the waves ebbing and flowing at the edge—like someone's life can get—always in motion without ever really going anywhere.

"Everyone at school is gonna know what I can do," Tara muttered.

"I'm not gonna tell," Flynn said.

"But there's Davis. He'll tell Bethany."

Flynn shook his head. "I don't know. Maybe, but you know they are also going to be pretty grateful. I'm thinking if you asked Davis . . . "

Tara nodded. "Maybe."

"Even if he tells, don't' sweat it," Flynn said. "Who'll believe him?"

Tara managed a smile. "Yeah. You're right. Who would believe him?"

Tara and Uncle Pat went to the hospital the next day, which was Sunday, to check on Bethany and Mrs. Pratt. Davis and his parents, as well as Bethany's parents, were there at her bedside, and when Davis saw Tara standing at the door, he jumped up from his chair and ran to meet her, then hugged her.

Tara was shocked by his friendliness. Then Davis turned and made the introduction.

"Everyone . . . this is Tara, the girl who saved Bet's life."

Bethany's parents swarmed her, engulfing her in hugs and praise that left Tara breathless.

Then Mr. Fanning put his hand in his pocket and pulled out a piece of paper and handed it to Tara.

"I was actually going to your house this afternoon, but you've saved me the trip. I've never been happier in my life than to be able to give you this. You've more than earned this, young lady."

Tara frowned. "Give me what?" she asked. Then her eyes widened in disbelief as she stared down at a check he'd written in her name, for more than fifty thousand dollars. It was the reward.

"Oh no, sir! I can't take this."

"Nonsense," Mr. Fanning said. "You earned it."

"But that's just it. I didn't really. I just . . . just . . . "

"Got lucky," Davis added. "You got lucky, but you did earn it."

Bethany sat up, then swung her legs off the side of the bed and motioned to Tara. "Hey, Luna . . . come here," she said.

Tara walked over to the bed, a little nervous as to what Davis must have said.

"Take it ... please," Bethany said, and closed Tara's fingers over the check she was still holding. "And just for the record, I'm so sorry we all treated you so bad before. I don't care how lunatic you get, there'll always be a place for you to sit with us at lunch."

College. All four years had just been paid for. All she had to do was graduate high school with a decent GPA.

Tara looked at Bethany and read what she was thinking. "People can think what they wanna think about what happened to you. You know Charlie didn't uh... touch you and that's enough. Your friends won't care one way or another. They're going to be happy you're alive and well."

Bethany's eyes filled with tears, but she was smiling.

"You are such a lunatic."

"Yeah. I know," Tara said, then turned around, noticed her uncle was standing back, looking a little ill at ease among some of Stillwater's social elite, and knew that wasn't right. "I am so forgetting my manners. Uncle Pat, this is Bethany. Bethany, my Uncle Pat."

Bethany smiled.

"I'm glad you're okay," Uncle Pat said.

Bethany looked up at Tara, then exhaled slowly. "Yeah ... I am okay, aren't I," she said. "Thanks to Tara."

"Mr. Carmichael, you have certainly raised an amazing girl," Johnson Breedlove said.

"Yes, I think so," Uncle Pat said.

Tara smiled with pride as she watched them including her uncle into the conversation.

What about me? I helped raise you, too.

Tara stifled a laugh. Who else could claim a ghost as a parent? She sighed, and then put the reward check into her pocket and slipped her hand into the crook of her uncle's arm. As she did, she felt a lighter, less firm pressure on her other arm. Henry—giving her his version of a ghostly hug, too. She sighed.

So ... considering everything, she might be a little bit amazing, after all.

EPILOGUE

On Monday Flynn met Tara at the front of the school, then walked with her into the building. He kept smiling at her as if he knew a big secret that she didn't.

"What?" she asked.

"Nothing," Flynn said, but he kept smiling as they walked up the steps and into the front door.

In the space of time it took for Tara's eyes to adjust to the change in light, she began to hear people clapping and saying her name.

"Luna. Luna. Luna."

"What's going on?" Tara cried.

Hundreds of students were lined up on both sides of the hall, clapping and shouting her name. Flynn looked at the expression on her face and then laughed.

"If you're all that psychic, you should have seen this coming."

Tara couldn't believe what she was seeing. Everyone was grinning at her and waving and shouting her name. She saw Nikki standing beside this tall, skinny kid with dark hair. Suddenly she realized it was Corey Palmer. It was the first time she'd seem him alive and in his own body. When he saw her looking, he gave her a thumbs up.

Then she saw Mac and Penny . . . and Mrs. Farmer and Coach Jones. And . . . even Mrs. Crabtree was smiling at her. This was unreal. She felt like giggling. Then she saw Prissy and Mel coming toward her.

"We're really sorry," Prissy said. "Bethany told us it was you who saved her life."

"Flynn and Davis were there, too," Tara said.

"We heard," Mel said. "Anyway . . . this is our way of

saying thanks," she added.

Tara felt like dancing. Maybe being the new kid at school her senior year wasn't going to be so bad after all. She glanced at Flynn. He was still grinning.

"Walk me to my locker?" she asked.

"I'll walk anywhere with you, Moon girl," he said softly, and together, they headed down the hall with everyone watching.

Tara felt like she was floating. Was this what Hollywood stars felt like as they walked the red carpet? Wow! What a great way to start a new week. Uncle Pat was cool with her 'stuff' and Bethany was alive. What more could a lunatic girl want?

Maybe . . . the location of DeeDee Broyles body?

That's right. Emmit! DeeDee! How was she going to convince Detectives Rutherford and Allen that she had another case for them to solve?

She sighed. How swiftly a bubble can burst.

Then she grinned. It was cool.

At last, she had a life.

What's Next in Tara's Lunatic Life?

THE LUNATIC DETECTIVE

Excerpt

Worms crawled between the eye sockets and over what had once been the bridge of her nose. The lower jaw had come loose from the joint and was drooping toward the breastplate, as if in eternal shock for the circumstance. The finger bones were curled as if she'd died in the middle of trying to dig her way out.

Tara stood above the newly opened grave, staring down in horror.

"Is that you, DeeDee?"

But DeeDee couldn't answer. There was the problem with her jaw.

All of a sudden, someone pushed Tara forward and she felt herself falling . . . falling . . . into the open grave . . . on top of what was left of poor DeeDee Broyles.

That was when she screamed.

Tara Luna sat straight up in bed, the sheet clutched beneath her chin as she stared wild-eyed around her bedroom, her heart pounding against her ribcage like a drum. All of a sudden, the loud roar of an engine swept past her window.

VVRRROOOMMM! VVRROOOMMM!!

She flinched, then relaxed when she saw the familiar silhouette of her uncle, Patrick Carmichael. She glanced at the clock, then groaned in disbelief as the roar of a lawn mower passed beneath her bedroom window again. It was just after eight a.m. on a Saturday! Couldn't he have waited a little longer before starting that thing up?

I think you'd look great as a red-head.

Tara rolled her eyes. Millicent! She'd just had the worst dream ever and was not in the mood for any input on hairstyles from the female ghost with whom she shared her life.

"I am not dying my hair," she announced, and swung her legs over to the side of the bed and stood up.

I was once a red-head . . . and a blonde . . . and a brunette.

Tara arched an eyebrow, but resisted commenting. She'd always suspected Millicent had been quite a swinger in her day because she was still way too focused on men.

"I'm going to shower," Tara announced, and headed for the bathroom across the hall. She opened the door just as Henry, the other ghost who shared her world, came floating by. Before she could stop herself, she'd walked through him.

"Eww! Henry! I hate when that happens!" she shrieked, and swiped at her face.

Henry didn't appear too pleased with her either, and vaporized himself in a huff.

He doesn't like to be displaced.

"Yeah, well I don't like to be slapped in the face with frozen spider webs, and that's what that feels like."

Interesting. I remember once when I was in France . . .

"OMG, Millicent. Please? I just woke up here."

A pinkish tinge suddenly flashed across Tara's line of vision, then she heard a very faint pop before Millicent's voice disappeared. "Oh great. Now she's ticked, too."

Still, finally glad to be alone, Tara closed the bathroom door behind her. Just because Henry and Millicent were no longer alive in the strict sense of the word, didn't mean she wanted them as company while she showered.

A short while later, she emerged, wide-awake and starving. She dashed across the hall to her room, dressing quickly in a pair of sweats and a new white tee from Stillwater, Oklahoma's world famous burger joint, Eskimo Joe's.

As she entered the kitchen, it was obvious from the amount of dirty dishes in the sink that Uncle Pat had already cooked breakfast. She began poking around, hoping he'd left some for her, and hoping it was regular food and not one of his experiments.

Her uncle had a tendency to mix things that didn't necessarily go good together. It was, he claimed, his way of 'going green,' by not wasting perfectly good food. If she could only convince him to quit stirring everything into one big pot to heat it up, she would be happy. She didn't mind eating left-overs. She just wanted to know what it used to be before she put it in her mouth.

As she passed by the sink, she saw a shot glass sitting inside a cereal bowl and stopped. This wasn't good. If Uncle Pat had already started drinking this early in the morning, the day was bound to go to hell before dark. Still, after she found a plate of food in the microwave that actually looked good, her mood lightened a little. She could smell sausage and potatoes, which went well together. She just hoped the yellow stuff on the side was scrambled eggs. He'd been known to try and pass off mashed squash on her before, claiming eggs and squash were both yellow and fluffy, so he failed to see her issue. She poked her finger into the food. It had the consistency of eggs. She licked her finger then grinned. Eggs!

"Bingo! Lucked out on this one," she said, and popped it in the microwave to heat. She poured herself a glass of juice and as soon as the microwave dinged, took her food and sat down to eat.

With the first couple of months of her senior year at a new school behind her, she was beginning to feel like she belonged. She'd gotten off on the wrong foot with one of the cheerleaders, which had resulted in some pretty hateful gossip and hazing. When that had started, Millicent had felt an obligation to retaliate on Tara's behalf. Flying dishes and ink pens had then shifted the gossip about Tara at Stillwater High to an all-out accusation that Tara Luna was not just a lunatic, but also a witch. She could handle being both a psychic and a medium, but a witch? How lame was that?

As she dug into her breakfast, she couldn't help thinking

about the one-eighty her life had taken after she'd used her psychic powers to figure out who had kidnaped Bethany Fanning, the head cheerleader of Stillwater High School. With the help of her new boyfriend, Flynn, and Bethany's boyfriend, Davis, they had managed to rescue Bethany just before she became fish food in Boomer Lake. Just thinking about Flynn O'Mara made her shiver. He was one smooth hottie.

All in all, it had been an eventful two months.

She was still eating when she sensed she was no longer alone. Since the sound of the mower was still going strong, it couldn't be Uncle Pat because he was still outside. She could also sense that whoever was here, wasn't mortal. She looked up, then over her shoulder.

When she saw the sad little ghost who'd come with the house they were renting, she sighed and pointed to a chair on the opposite side of the table.

"Hey, DeeDee. Have a seat. I had a dream about you last night. I've been waiting for you to come back. We need to talk."

DeeDee drifted past the chair Tara had indicated, choosing instead to hover near the doorway.

"Okay, here's the deal," Tara said, as she chewed. "Millicent explained your situation to me. I know you used to live in this house. I know you were also murdered here. I also know there was never an investigation into your murder because no one reported you missing . . . which leads me to the question, why not?"

DeeDee didn't have an answer, which usually meant she didn't know it. Spirits were often confused after they died. Sometimes they did not understand what had happened to them, or where they were supposed to be. Tara knew that after the traditional 'passing into the light,' they could come back and forth if they wished. But she suspected DeeDee had never crossed over. Ever. Which she found really sad.

"I'm really sorry that I don't have any answers for you, yet. But you already know I'm having problems with your brother, Emmit."

When DeeDee suddenly went from passive to a dark, angry shadow, Tara flinched. Talk about being in a mood. DeeDee was certainly in one now.

"So, what do you suggest?" Tara asked.

The dark shadow swirled to the ceiling and then down to the floor, like a puppet dancing on a string.

"That is not a helpful answer," Tara muttered, and scooped another bite into her mouth, her eyes narrowing thoughtfully as she chewed. "Here's the deal. I've already done a lot of legwork on this mystery. I found out you and Emmit once owned this house together, although he totally denies he ever had a sister."

At that news, the dark shadow bounced from one end of the kitchen to the other, rattling dishes in the cabinets.

"Easy," Tara cautioned. "No breaking dishes, please. I also found out where he lives now. You know I went to see him, which opened up this huge can of worms. Something I said to him set him off in a big way because now he's stalking me."

The dark shadow shifted back to DeeDee's ghost again, drifting about a foot above the floor like dandelion puffs floating in the wind.

"But you already knew that, too, so don't play dumb," Tara muttered. "And, I thank you again for scaring him off before he found me here the other day." She frowned. "However, I still can't figure out how he got a key to this house. There's no way the lock on the front door is still the one from back when you guys owned the house. Your freaky brother either picked the lock, or had some kind of master key. Either way, he scared the you-know-what out of me . . . digging through all our closets and stuff. I don't even want to think about what he would have done to me if he'd found me hiding in the back of Uncle Pat's closet. Like I said before, I owe you . . . scaring him off like that. But!" She pointed her fork at DeeDee. "Did you know he's stalking me *outside* of the house, too?"

Tara felt the little ghost's empathy as if she'd been hugged. "Yes, well, I'm sorry, too. Thanks to you and Millicent, I've managed to get away from him both times, but my luck can't hold forever. If only you could tell me where your body is buried, it would open an investigation and the guilty party, whom I suspect is your brother Emmit, would be caught."

Like before, an image of upturned earth and a pile of leaves flashed through Tara's mind.

"Okay. I get that the killer dug a hole, and that it was probably in the fall, because there were leaves all over the ground. But where? No. Wait. I know you were buried in the back yard." Then she grimaced. "Imagine my joy in learning that. What I meant was, I don't know where in the back yard."

Another image of the backyard flashed in Tara's mind. It was like looking at a postcard someone had sent her. In this instance, the postcard had come from DeeDee.

"I already know it's in our backyard. But it's huge. I can't just start digging holes. I don't know how deep the hole was where you were buried, or where to start looking."

Sadness swept through Tara so fast that she was crying before she knew it.

"Oh, DeeDee," Tara whispered, as she swiped at the tears on her cheeks. "I'm not giving up. I'm just talking out loud."

Within the space of a heartbeat, she found herself alone.

"Bummer," Tara muttered. "What a way to start the weekend."

ABOUT SHARON SALA

Sharon Sala's stories are often dark, dealing with the realities of this world, and yet she's able to weave hope and love within the words for the readers who clamor for her latest works.

Her books repeatedly make the big lists, including The New York *Times*, *USA Today*, *Publisher's Weekly* and Waldenbooks Mass market fiction, and she's been nominated for a RITA seven times, which is the romance writer's equivalent of having an OSCAR or an EMMY nomination.

Always an optimist in the face of bad times, many of the stories she writes come to her in dreams, but there's nothing fanciful about her work. She puts her faith in God, still trusts in love and the belief that, no matter what, everything comes full circle.

Visit her at http://sharonsalabooks.com and on Facebook.

CPSIA information can be obtained at www.ICGtesting.com
Printed in the USA
LVOW090741221011

251527LV00001B/25/P